FICTION HOUSE PRESS PRESENTS

MANHUNT

July 1953
Vol. 1, No. 7

This reprint edition is a facsimile of the original pulp magazine. Variations in printing and quality can be attributed to the original magazine which was printed on rough woodpulp paper. No attempt has been made to politically correct any language deemed inappropriate to the modern reader.

ISBN 978-1-64720-670-3

www.FictionHousePress.com
fictionhousepress@gmail.com

VOL. 1, NO. 7

MANHUNT

JULY, 1953

CONTENTS

MANHUNT VOLUME 1, NUMBER 7, JULY, 1953. Single copies 35 cents. Subscriptions $4.00 for one year in the United States and Possessions; elsewhere $5.00 (in U. S. funds) for one year. Published monthly by Flying Eagle Publications, Inc. (an affiliate of St. John Publishing Company), 545 Fifth Avenue, New York 17, New York. Telephone MU 7-6623.

The Wench is Dead

Howie was innocent, but that didn't matter. He was a skid-row bum, and he'd been in Mamie's room the morning she was murdered.

A Novelette

BY FREDRIC BROWN

A FUZZ is a fuzz is a fuzz when you awaken from a wino jag. God, I'd drunk three pints of muscatel that I know of and maybe more, maybe lots more, because that's when I drew a blank, that's when research stopped. I rolled over on the cot so I could look out through the dirty pane of the window at the clock in the hockshop across the way.

Ten o'clock said the clock.

Get up, Howard Perry, I told myself. Get up, you B. A. S. for bastard, rise and greet the day. Hit the floor and get moving if you want to keep that job, that all-important job that keeps you drinking and sometimes eating and sometimes sleeping with Billie the Kid when she hasn't got a sucker on the hook. That's your life, you B.A.S., you bastard. That's your life for a while. This is it, this is the McCoy, this is the way a wino meets the not-so-newborn day. You're learning, man.

Pull on a sock, another sock, pants, shirt, shoes, get the hell to Burke's and wash a dish, wash a thousand dishes for six bits an hour and a meal or two a day when you want it.

God, I thought,

did I really have the habit? Nuts, not in three months. Not when you've been a normal drinker all your life. Not when, much as you've always enjoyed drinking, it's always been in moderation and you've always been able to handle the stuff. This was just temporary.

And I had only a few weeks to go. In a few weeks I'd be back in Chicago, back at my desk in my father's investment company, back wearing white shirts, and B.A.S. would stand for Bachelor of Arts in Sociology. That was a laugh right now, that degree. Three months ago it had meant something — but that was in Chicago, and this was L.A., and now all it meant was bastard. That's all it had meant ever since I started drifting.

It's funny, the way those things can happen. You've got a good family and a good education, and then suddenly, for no reason you can define, you start drifting. You lose interest in your family and your job, and one day you find yourself headed for the Coast.

You sit down one day and ask yourself how it happened. But you can't answer. There are a thousand little answers, sure, but there's no *big* answer. It's easier to worry about where the next bottle of sweet wine is coming from.

And that's when you realize your own personal B.A.S. stands for bastard.

With me, L.A. had been the end of the line. I'd seen the *Dishwasher Wanted* sign in Burke's window, and suddenly I'd known what I had to do. At pearl-diver's wages, it would take a long time to get up the bus fare back to Chicago and family and respectability, but that was beside the point. The point was that after a hundred thousand dirty dishes there'd *be* a bus ticket to Chicago.

But it had been hard to remember the ticket and forget the dishes. Wine is cheap, but they're not giving it away. Since I'd started pearl-diving I'd had grub and six bits an hour for seven hours a day. Enough to drink on and to pay for this dirty, crumby little crackerbox of a room.

So here I was, still thinking about the bus ticket, and still on my uppers on East Fifth Street, L.A. Main Street used to be the tenderloin street of Los Angeles and I'd headed for it when I jumped off the freight, but I'd found that the worst district, the real skid row, was now on Fifth Street in the few blocks east of Main. The worst the district, the cheaper the living, and that's what I'd been looking for.

Sure, by Fifth Street standards, I was being a pantywaist to hold down a steady job like that, but sleeping in doorways was a little too rugged and I'd found out quickly that panhandling wasn't for me. I lacked the knack.

I dipped water from the cracked basin and rubbed it on my face, and the feel of the stubble told me I could get by one more day without shaving. Or anyway I could wait till evening so the shave would be fresh in case I'd be sleeping with Billie.

Cold water helped a little but I still felt like hell. There were empty wine bottles in the corner and I checked to make sure they were completely empty, and they were. So were my pockets, except, thank God, for tobacco and cigarette papers. I rolled myself a cigarette and lighted it.

But I needed a drink to start the day.

What does a wino do when he wakes up broke (and how often does he wake otherwise?) and needs a drink? Well, I'd found several answers to that. The easiest one, right now, would be to hit Billie for a drink if she was awake yet, and alone.

I crossed the street to the building where Billie had a room. A somewhat newer building, a hell of a lot nicer room, but then she paid a hell of a lot more for it.

I rapped on her door softly, a little code knock we had. If she wasn't awake she wouldn't hear it and if she wasn't alone she wouldn't answer it.

But she called out, "It's not locked; come on in," and she said "Hi, Professor," as I closed the door behind me. "Professor" she called me, occasionally and banteringly. It was my way of talking, I guess. I'd tried at first to use poor diction, bad grammar, to fit in with the place, but I'd given it up as too tough a job. Besides, I'd learned Fifth Street already had quite a bit of good grammar. Some of its denizens had been newspapermen once, some had written poetry; one I knew was a defrocked clergyman.

I said, "Hi, Billie the Kid."

"Just woke up, Howie. What time is it?"

"A little after ten," I told her. "Is there a drink around?"

"Jeez, only ten? Oh well, I had seven hours. Guy came here when Mike closed at two, but he didn't stay long."

She sat up in bed and stretched, the covers falling away from her naked body. Beautiful breasts she had, size and shape of half grapefruits and firm. Nice arms and shoulders, and a lovely face. Hair black and sleek in a page-boy bob that fell into place as she shook her head. Twenty-five, she told me once; and I believed her, but she could have passed for several years less than that, even now without make up and her eyes still a little puffy from sleep. Certainly it didn't show that she'd spent three years as a B-girl, part-time hustler, heavy drinker. Before that she'd been married to a man who'd worked for a manufacturing jeweler; he'd suddenly left for parts unknown with a considerable portion of his employer's stock, leaving Billie in a jam and with a mess of debts.

Wilhelmina Kidder, Billie the Kid, my Billie. Any man's Billie if he flashed a roll, but oddly I'd found that I could love her a little and not let that bother me. Maybe because it had been that way when I'd first met her over a month ago; I'd come to love her knowing what she was, so why should it bother me? What she saw in me I don't know, and didn't care.

"About that drink," I said.

She laughed and threw down the covers, got out of bed and walked past me naked to the closet to get a robe. I wanted to reach for her but I didn't; I'd learned by now that Billie the Kid was never amorous early in the morning and resented any passes made before noon.

She shrugged into a quilted robe and padded barefoot over to the little refrigerator behind the screen that hid a tiny kitchenette. She opened the door and said, "God damn it."

"God damn what?" I wanted to know. "Out of liquor?"

She held up over the screen a Hiram Walker bottle with only half an inch of ready-mixed Manhattan in it. Almost the only thing Billie ever drank, Manhattans.

"As near out as matters. Honey, would you run upstairs and see if Mame's got some? She usually has."

Mame is a big blonde who works behind the bar at Mike Karas' joint, The Best Chance, where Billie works as B-girl. A tough number, Mame. I said, "If she's asleep she'll murder me for waking her. What's wrong with the store?"

"She's up by now. She was off early last night. And if you get it at the store it won't be on ice. Wait, I'll phone her, though, so if she *is* asleep it'll be me that wakes her and not you."

She made the call and then nodded. "Okay, honey. She's got a full bottle she'll lend me. Scram."

I scrammed, from the second floor rear to the third floor front. Mame's door was open; she was out in the hallway paying off a milkman and waiting for him to receipt the bill. She said, "Go on in. Take a load off." I went inside the room and sat down in the chair that was built to match Mame, overstuffed. I ran my fingers around under the edge of the cushion; one of Mame's men friends might have sat there with change in his pocket. It's surprising how much change you can pick up just by trying any overstuffed chairs or sofas you sit on. No change this time, but I came up with a fountain pen, a cheap dime-store-looking one. Mame had just closed the door and I held it up. "In the chair. Yours, Mame?"

"Nope. Keep it, Howie, I got a pen."

"Maybe one of your friends'll miss it," I said. It was too cheap a pen to sell or hock so I might as well be honest about it.

"Nope, I know who lost it. Seen it in his pocket last night. It was Jesus, and the hell with him."

"Mame, you sound sacrilegious."

She laughed. "Hay-*soos*, then. Jesus Gonzales. A Mex. But when he told me that was his handle I called him Jesus. And Jesus was *he* like a cat on a hot stove!" She walked around me over to her refrigerator but her voice kept on. "Told me not to turn on the lights when he come in and went over to watch out the front window for a while like he was watching for the heat. Looks out my side window too, one with the fire escape. Pulls down all the shades before he says okay, turn on the lights." The refrigerator door closed and she came back with a bottle.

"Was he a hot one," she said. "Just got his coat off — he threw it on that chair, when there's a knock. Grabs his coat again and goes out my side window down the fire escape." She laughed again. "Was that a flip? It was only Dixie from the next room knocking, to bum cigarettes. So if I ever see Jesus again it's no dice, guy as jumpy as that. Keep his pen. Want a drink here?"

"If you'll have one with me."

"I don't drink, Howie. Just keep stuff around for friends and callers. Tell Billie to give me another bottle like this back. I got a friend likes Manhattans, like her."

When I got back to Billie's room, she'd put on a costume instead of the robe, but it wasn't much of a costume. A skimpy Bikini bathing suit. She pirouetted in it. "Like it, Howie? Just bought it yesterday."

"Nice," I said, "but I like you better without it."

"Pour us drinks, huh? For me, just a quickie."

"Speaking of quickies," I said.

She picked up a dress and started to pull it over her head. "If you're thinking that way, Professor, I'll hide the family treasures. Say, that's a good line; I'm getting to talk like you do sometimes."

I poured us drinks and we sat down with them. She'd stepped into sandals and was dressed. I said, "You've got lots of good lines, Billie the Kid. But correct me — was that lingerie instead of a bathing suit, or am I out of date on fashions?"

"I'm going to the beach today, Howie, for a sun-soak. Won't go near the water so why not just wear the suit under and save changing? Say, why don't you take a day off and come along?"

"Broke. The one thing to be said for Burke as an employer is that he pays every day. Otherwise there'd be some dry, dry evenings."

"What you make there? A fin, maybe. I'll lend you a fin."

"That way lies madness," I said. "Drinks I'll take from you, or more important things than drinks. But taking money would make me —" I stopped and wondered just what taking money from Billie would make me, just how consistent I was being. After all, I could always send it back to her from Chicago. What kept me from taking it, then? A gal named Honor, I guess. Corny as it sounds, I said it lightly. "I could not love thee, dear, so much, loved I not Honor more."

"You're a funny guy, Howie. I don't understand you."

Suddenly I wanted to change the

subject. "Billie, how come Mame doesn't drink?"

"Don't you know hypes don't like to drink?"

"Sure, but I didn't spot Mame for one."

"Hype with a big H for heroin, Howie. Doesn't show it much, though. I'll give you that."

"I haven't known enough junkies to be any judge," I said. "The only one I know for sure is the cook at Burke's."

"Don't ever try it, Howie. It's bad stuff. I joy-popped once just to see what it was like, but never again. Too easy to get to like it. And Howie, it can make things rough."

I said, "I hear your words of wisdom and shall stick to drink. Speaking of which —" I poured myself another.

2

I got to the restaurant — it's on Main a block from Fifth — at a quarter after eleven, only fifteen minutes late. Burke was at the stove — he does his own cooking until noon, when Ramon comes on — and turned to glare at me but didn't say anything.

Still feeling good from the drinks, I dived into my dishwashing.

The good feeling was mostly gone, though, by noon, when Ramon came on. He had a fresh bandage on his forehead; I wondered if there was a new knife wound under it. He already had two knife scars, old ones, on his cheek and on his chin. He looked mean, too, and I decided to stay out of his way. Ramon's got a nasty temper when he needs a jolt, and it was pretty obvious that he needed one. He looked like a man with a kingsize monkey, and he was. I'd often wondered how he fed it. Cooks draw good money compared to other restaurant help, but even a cook doesn't get enough to support a five or six cap a day habit, not at a joint like Burke's anyway. Ramon was tall for a Mexican, but he was thin and his face looked gaunt. It's an ugly face except when he grins and his teeth flash white. But he wouldn't be grinning this afternoon, not if he needed a jolt.

Burke went front to work the register and help at the counter for the noon rush, and Ramon took over at the stove. We worked in silence until the rush was over, about two o'clock.

He came over to me then. He was sniffling and his eyes were running. He said, "Howie, you do me a favor. I'm burning, Howie, I need a fix, quick. I got to sneak out, fifteen minutes."

"Okay, I'll try to watch things. What's working?"

"Two hamburg steak dinners on. Done one side, five more minutes other side. You know what else to put on."

"Sure, and if Burke comes back I'll tell him you're in the can. But you'd better hurry."

He rushed out, not even bothering to take off his apron or chef's hat.

I timed five minutes on the clock and then I took up the steaks, added the trimmings and put them on the ledge, standing at an angle back of the window so Burke couldn't see that it was I and not Ramon who was putting them there. A few minutes later the waitress put in a call for stuffed peppers, a pair; they were already cooked and I didn't have any trouble dishing them.

Ramon came back before anything else happened. He looked like a different man — he would be for as long as the fix lasted. His teeth flashed. "Million thanks, Howie." He handed me a flat pint bottle of muscatel. "For you, my friend."

"Ramon," I said, "you are a gentleman and a scholar." He went back to his stove and started scraping it. I bent down out of sight to open the bottle. I took a good long drink and then hid it back out of sight under one of the tubs.

Two-thirty, and my half-hour lunch break. Only I wasn't hungry. I took another drink of the muskie and put it back. I could have killed it but the rest of the afternoon would go better if I rationed it and made it last until near quitting time.

I wandered over to the alley entrance, rolling a cigarette. A beautiful bright day out; it would have been wonderful to be at the beach with Billie the Kid.

Only Billie the Kid wasn't at the beach; she was coming toward me from the mouth of the alley. She was still wearing the dress she'd pulled on over the bathing suit but she wasn't at the beach. She was walking toward me, looking worried, looking frightened.

I walked to meet her. She grabbed my arm, tightly. "Howie. Howie, did you kill Mame?"

"Did I — *what?*"

Her eyes were big, looking up at me. "Howie, if you did, I don't care. I'll help you, give you money to get away. But —"

"Whoa," I said, "Whoa, Billie. I didn't kill Mame. I didn't even rape her. She was okay when I left. What happened? Or are you dreaming this up?"

"She's dead, Howie, murdered. And about the time you were there. They found her a little after noon and say she'd been dead somewhere around two hours. Let's go have a drink and I'll tell you what all happened."

"All right," I said. "I've got most of my lunch time left. Only I haven't been paid yet —"

"Come on, hurry." As we walked out of the alley she took a bill from her purse and stuffed it into my pocket. We took the nearest gin-mill and ordered drinks at a booth at the back where we weren't near enough anyone to be heard. The bill she'd put in my pocket was a sawbuck. When the waitress brought our drinks and the change I shoved it toward Billie. She shook her head and pushed it back. "Keep it and owe me ten, Howie. You might need it in case — well, just in case." I said, "Okay, Billie, but I'll pay this back." I would, too, but it probably wouldn't be until I mailed it to her from Chicago and it would probably surprise the hell out of her to get it.

I said, "Now tell me, but quit looking so worried. I'm as innocent as new-fallen snow — and I don't mean cocaine. Let me reconstruct my end first, and then tell yours. I got to work at eleven-twenty. Walked straight there from your place, so it would have been ten after when I left you. And — let's see, from the other end, it was ten o'clock when I woke up, wouldn't have been over ten or fifteen minutes before I knocked on your door, another few minutes before I got to Mame's and I was up there only a few minutes. Say I saw her last around twenty after ten, and she was okay then. Over."

"Huh? Over what?"

"I mean, you take it. From when I left you, about ten minutes after eleven."

"Oh. Well, I straightened the room, did a couple things, and left, it must have been a little after twelve on account of the noon whistles had blown just a few minutes ago. I was going to the beach. I was going to walk over to the terminal and catch the Santa Monica bus, go to Ocean Park. Only first I stopped in the drugstore right on the corner for a cup of coffee. I was there maybe ten-fifteen minutes letting it cool enough to drink and drinking it. While I was there I heard a cop car stop near but I didn't think anything of it; they're always picking up drunks and all.

"But while I was there too I remembered I'd forgot to bring my sun glasses and sun-tan oil, so I went back to get them.

"Minute I got inside the cops were waiting and they asked if I lived there and then started asking questions, did I know Mame and when I saw her last and all."

"Did you tell them you'd talked to her on the phone?"

"Course not, Howie. I'm not a dope. I knew by then something had happened to her and if I told them about that call and what it was about, it would have brought you in and put you on the spot. I didn't even tell them you were with me, let alone going up to Mame's. I kept you out of it.

"They're really questioning everybody, Howie. They didn't pull me in but they kept me in my own room questioning me till just fifteen minutes ago. See, they really worked on me because I admitted I knew Mame — I had to admit that 'cause we work at the same place and they'd have found that out.

"And of course they knew she was a hype, her arms and all; they're checking everybody's arms and thank God mine are okay. They asked me mostly about where we worked, Mike's. I think they figure Mike Karas is a dealer, what with Mame working for him."

"Is he, Billie?"

"I don't know, honey. He's in some racket, but it isn't dope."

I said, "Well, I don't see what either of us has to worry about. It's not our — My God, I just remembered something."

"What, Howie?"

"A guy saw me going in her room, a milkman. Mame was in the hall paying him off when I went up. She told me to go on in and I did, right past him."

"Jesus, Howie, did she call you by name when she told you to go on in? If they get a name, even a first name, and you living right across the street —"

I thought hard. "Pretty sure she didn't, Billie. She told me to go in and take a load off, but I'm pretty sure she didn't add a Howie to it. Anyway, they may never find the milkman was there. He isn't likely to stick his neck out by coming to them. How was she killed, Billie?"

"Somebody said a shiv, but I don't know for sure."

"Who found her and how come?"

"I don't know. They were asking me questions, not me asking them. That part'll be in the papers, though."

"All right," I said. "Let's let it go till this evening, then. How's about this evening, Billie, are you going to The Best Chance anyway?"

"I *got* to, tonight, after that. If I don't show up, they'll want to know why and where I was and everything. And listen, don't you come around either, after hours tonight or in the morning. You stay away from that building, Howie. If they find that milkman they might even have him staked out watching for you. Don't even walk *past*. You better even stay off that block, go in and out the back way to your own room. And we better not even see each other till the heat's off or till we know what the score is."

I sighed.

I was ten minutes late reporting back and Burke glared at me again but still didn't say anything. I guess I was still relatively dependable for a dishwasher, but I was learning.

I made the rest of the wine last me till Baldy, the evening shift dishwasher, showed up to relieve me. Burke paid me off for the day then, and I was rich again.

3

Someone was shaking me, shaking me hard. I woke to fuzz and fog and Billie the Kid was peering through it at me, looking really scared, more scared than when she'd asked me yesterday if I'd killed Mame.

"Howie, wake up." I was in my own little shoe-box of a room, Billie standing by my cot bending over me. I wasn't covered, but the extent of my undressing had been to kick off my shoes.

"Howie, listen, you're in trouble, honey. You got to get out of here, back way like I come in. Hurry."

I sat up and wanted to know the time.

"Only nine, Howie. But hurry. Here. This will help you." She screwed off the top of a half pint bottle of whisky. "Drink some quick. Help you wake up."

I took a drink and the whisky burned rawly down my throat. For a moment I thought it was going to make me sick to my stomach, but then it decided to stay down and it did clear my head a little. Not much, but a little.

"What's wrong, Billie?"

"Put on your shoes. I'll tell you, but not here."

Luckily my shoes were loafers and I could step into them. I went to the basin of water, rubbed some on my face. While I washed and dried and ran a comb through my hair Billie was going through the dresser; a towel on the bed, everything I owned piled on it. It didn't make much of a bundle.

She handed it to me and then was pulling me out into the hallway, me and everything I owned. Apparently I wasn't coming back here, or Billie didn't think I was.

Out into the alley, through to Sixth Street and over Sixth to Main, south on Main. A restaurant with booths, mostly empty. The waitress came over and I ordered coffee, black. Billie ordered ham and eggs and toast and when the waitress left she leaned across the table. "I didn't want to argue with her in front of you, Howie, but that food I ordered is for you; you're going to eat it all. You got to be sober."

I groaned, but knew it would be easier to eat than to argue with a Billie the Kid as vehement as this one.

"What is it, Billie? What's up?"

"Did you read the papers last night?"

I shook my head. I hadn't read any papers up to about nine o'clock and after that I didn't remember what I'd done or hadn't. But I wouldn't have read any papers. That reminded me to look in my pockets to see what money I had left, if any. No change, but thank God there were some crumpled bills. A five and two ones, when I pulled them out and looked under cover of the table. I'd had a little over nine out of the ten Billie had given me to buy us a drink with, a little under five I'd got from Burke. That made fourteen and I'd spent seven of it somehow — and God knows how since I couldn't possibly have drunk that much muskie or even that much whisky at Fifth Street prices. But at least I hadn't been rolled, so it could have been worse.

"They got that milkman, Howie," Billie was saying. "Right off. He'd given Mame a receipt and she'd dropped it on that little table by the door so they knew he'd been there and they found him and he says he'll know you if he sees you. He described you too. You thinking straight by now, Howie?"

"Sure I'm thinking straight. What if they *do* find me? Damn it, I didn't kill her. Didn't have any reason to. They can't do any more than question me."

"Howie, haven't you ever been in trouble with cops? Not on anything serious, I guess, or you wouldn't talk like that. That milkman would put you right on the scene at close to the right time and that's all they'd want. They got nobody else to work on.

"Sure they'll question you. With fists and rubber hoses they'll question you. They'll beat the hell out of you for days on end, tie you in a chair with five hundred watts in your eyes and slap you every time you close them. Sure they'll question you. They'll question you till you wish you *had* killed Mame so you could tell 'em and get it over with and get some sleep. Howie, cops are tough, mean bastards when they're trying to pin down a murder rap. This is a murder rap, Howie."

I smiled a little without meaning to. Not because what she'd been saying was funny, but because I was thinking of the headlines if they did beat the truth out of me, or if I had to tell all to beat the rap. *Chicago Scion in Heroin Murder Case.* Chicago papers please copy.

I saw the hurt look on Billie's face and straightened mine. "Sorry," I said. "I was laughing at something else. Go on."

But the waitress was coming and Billie waited till she'd left. She shoved the ham and eggs and toast in front of me. "Eat," she said. I ate.

"And that isn't all, Howie. They'll frame you on some other charge to hold you. Howie, they might even frame you on the murder rap itself if they don't find who else did it. They could do it easy, just take a few little things from her room — it had been searched — and claim you had 'em on you or they were in your room. How'd you prove they weren't? And what'd your word be against a cop's? They could put you in the the little room and gas you, Howie. And there's something else, too."

"Something worse that *that?*"

"I don't mean that. I mean what they'd do to me, Howie. And that'd be for *sure.* A perjury rap, a nice long one. See, I signed a statement after they questioned me, and that'd make it perjury for me if you tell 'em the truth about why you went up to see Mame. And what else could you tell them?"

I put down my knife and fork and stared at her. I hadn't been *really* worried about the things she'd been telling me. Innocent men, I'd been telling myself, aren't framed by the cops on murder charges. Not if they're willing to tell the truth down the line. They might give me a bad time, I thought, but they wouldn't hold me long if I leveled with them. But if Billie had signed a statement, then telling them the truth was out. Billie was on the wrong side of the law already; they *would* take advantage of perjury to put her away, maybe for several years.

I said, "I'm sorry, Billie. I didn't realize I'd have to involve you if I had to tell them the truth."

"Eat, Howie. Eat all that grub. Don't worry about me; I just mentioned it. You're in worse trouble than *I* am. But I'm glad you're talking straight; you sound really awake now. Now you go on eating and I'll tell you what you've got to do.

"First, this milkman's description. Height, weight and age fairly close but not exact on any, and anyway you can't change that. But you got to change clothes, buy new ones, because Jesus, the guy got your clothes perfect. Blue denim shirt cut off above elbows, tan work pants, brown loafers. Now first thing when you leave here, buy different clothes, see?"

"All right," I said. "How else did he describe me?"

"Well, he thought you had blond hair and it's a little darker than that, not much. Said you needed a shave — you need one worse now — and said you looked like a Fifth Street bum, a wino maybe. That's all, except he's sure he could identify you if he ever saw you again. And that's bad, Howie."

"It is," I said.

"Howie, do you want to blow town? I can lend you — well, I'm a little low right now and on account of Karas' place being watched so close I won't be able to pick up any extra money for a while, but I can lend you fifty if you want to blow town. Do you?"

"No, Billie," I said. "I don't want to blow town. Not unless you want to go with me."

God, what had made me say *that?* What had I meant by it? What business had I taking Billie away from the district she knew, the place where she could make a living — if I couldn't — putting her further in a jam for disappearing when she was more or less a witness in a murder case? And when I wanted to be back in Chicago, back working for my father and being respectable, within a few weeks anyway.

What had I meant? I couldn't take Billie back with me, much as I liked — maybe loved — her. Billie the Kid as the wife of a respectable investment man? It wouldn't work, for either of us. But if I hadn't meant that, what the hell *had* I meant?

But Billie was shaking her head. "Howie, it wouldn't work. Not for us, not right now. If you could quit drinking, straighten out. But I know — I know you can't. It isn't your fault and — oh, honey, let's not talk about that now. Anyway, I'm *glad* you don't want to lam because — well, because I *am*. But listen —"

"Yes, Billie?"

"You've got to change the way you look — just a little. Buy a different colored shirt, see? And different pants, shoes instead of loafers. Get a haircut — you need one anyway so get a short one. Then get a hotel room — off Fifth Street. Main is okay if you stay away from Fifth.

And shave — you had a stubble when that milkman saw you. How much money you got left?"

"Seven," I said. "But that ought to do it. I don't need *new* clothes; I can swap with uncle."

"You'll need more than that. Here." It was a twenty.

"Thanks, Billie. I owe you thirty." Owe her thirty? Hell, how much did I owe Billie the Kid already, outside of money, things money can't buy? I said, "And how'll we get in touch with one another? You say I shouldn't come to your place. Will you come to mine, tonight?"

"I — I guess they won't be suspicious if I take a night off, Howie, as long as it wasn't that first night. Right after the — after what happened to Mame. All right, Howie. You know a place called The Shoebox on Main up across from the court house?"

"I know where it is."

"I'll meet you there tonight at eight. And — and stay in your room, wherever you take one, till then. And — and try to stay sober, Howie."

4

It shouldn't be hard, I thought, to stay sober when you're scared. And I was scared, now.

I stayed on Main Street, away from Fifth, and I did the things Billie had suggested. I bought a tan work shirt, and changed it right in the store where I bought it for the blue one I'd been wearing. I stopped in the barber school place for a four-bit haircut and, while I was at it, a two-bit shave. I had one idea Billie hadn't thought of; I spent a buck on a used hat. I hadn't been wearing one and a hat makes a man look different. At a shoe repair shop that handled used shoes I traded in my loafers and a dollar fifty for a pair of used shoes. I decided not to worry about the trousers; their color wasn't distinctive.

I bought newspapers; I wanted to read for myself everything Billie had told me about the murder, and there might be other details she hadn't mentioned. Some wine too, but just a pint to sip on. I was going to stay sober, but it would be a long boring day waiting for my eight o'clock date with Billie the Kid.

I registered double at a little walk-up hotel on Market Street around the corner from Main, less than a block from the place of my evening date. She'd be coming with me, of course, since we wouldn't dare go to her place, and I didn't want there to be even a chance of trouble in bringing her back with me. Not that trouble would be likely in a place like that but I didn't want even the minor trouble of having to change the registration from single to double if the clerk saw us coming in, not for fifty cents difference in the price of the room.

I sipped at the wine slowly and read the papers. The *Mirror* gave it the best coverage, with pictures. A picture of Mame that must have been found in her room and that had been taken at least ten years ago — she looked to be in her late teens or early twenties — a flashlight shot of the interior of her room, but taken after her body had been removed, and an exterior of The Best Chance, where she'd worked. But, even from the *Mirror*, I didn't learn anything Billie hadn't told me, except Mame's full name and just how and when the body had been discovered. The time had been 12:05, just about the time Billie was leaving from her room on the floor below. The owner of the building had dropped around, with tools, to fix a dripping faucet Mame (Miss Mamie Gaynor, 29) had complained about the day before. When he'd knocked long enough to decide she wasn't home he'd let himself in with his duplicate key. The milkman's story and the description he'd given of me was exactly as Billie had given them.

I paced up and down the little room, walked the worn and shabby carpet, wondering. Was there — short of the sheer accident of my running into that milkman — any danger of my being picked up just from that description? No, surely not. It was accurate as far as it went, but it was too vague, could fit too many men in this district, for anyone to think of me in connection with it. And now, with a change of clothes, a shave, wearing a hat outdoors, I doubted if the milkman would recognize me. I couldn't remember his face; why would he remember mine? And there was no tie-in otherwise, except through Billie. Nobody but Billie knew that I'd even met Mame. The only two times I'd ever seen her had been in Billie's place when she'd dropped in while I was there, once for only a few minutes, once for an hour or so. And one other time I'd been up to her room, that time to borrow cigarettes for Billie; it had been very late, after stores and bars were closed.

The fact that I'd disappeared from my room in that block? That would mean nothing. Tomorrow a week's rent was due; the landlord would come to collect it, find me and my few possessions gone, and rent it again. He'd think nothing of it. Why should he?

No, now that I'd taken the few precautions Billie had suggested, I was safe enough as long as I stayed away from her building.

Why was I hiding here now, then?

The wine was gone and I wanted more. But I knew what shape I'd be in by eight o'clock if I kept on drinking it, starting at this hour of the morning.

But I'd go nuts if I stayed here, doing nothing. I picked up the papers, read the funny sheets, a few other things. Back in the middle of one of them a headline over a short item caught my eye, I don't know for what reason. *Victim in Alley Slaying Identified.*

Maybe my eye had first caught the name down in the body of the story, Jesus Gonzales. And Mame's jittery guest of the night before her death had been named Jesus Gonzales.

I read the story. Yesterday morning at dawn the body of a man had been found in an areaway off Winston Street near San Pedro Street. He had been killed with a blunt instrument, probably a blackjack. As he had been robbed of everything he was carrying, no identification had been made at first. Now he had been identified as Jesus Gonzales, 41, of Mexico City, D. F. He had arrived in Los Angles the day before on the S. S. Guadalajara, out of Tokyo. His passport, which had been left in his room at the Berengia Hotel, and other papers left with it, showed that he had been in the Orient on a buying trip for a Mexico City art object importing firm in which he was a partner, and that he was stopping in Los Angeles for a brief vacation on his return trip.

Mame's Jesus Gonzales? It certainly looked that way. The place and time fitted; less than two blocks from her room. So did the time, the morning after he'd been frightened by that knock at the door and had left unceremoniously via the fire escape.

But why would he have hooked up with Mame? The Berengia is a swank hotel, only people with well-lined pockets stay there. Mame was no prize; at the Berengia he could have done better through his own bellhop.

Or could it be a factor that Mame was a junkie and, stopping in at The Best Chance, he'd recognized her as one and picked her for that reason? He could have been a hype himself, in need of a jolt and in a city where he had no contacts, or — and this seemed even more likely because of his just having landed from Tokyo — he'd smuggled some dope in with him and was looking for a dealer to sell it. The simplest and safest way to find a dealer would be through an addict.

It was just a wild guess, of course, but it wasn't too wild to be possible. And damn it, Mame's Jesus Gonzales *had* acted suspiciously and he *had* been afraid of something. Maybe he'd thought somebody was following him, following him and Mame home from The Best Chance. If he was the same Jesus Gonzales who'd just been killed and robbed only two blocks from her place, then he'd been dead right in being careful. He'd made his mistake in assuming that the knocker on Mame's door was the man who'd followed him and in going down the fire escape. Maybe his *Nemesis* had still been outside the building, probably watching from across the street, and had seen him leave. And on Winston Street *Nemesis* had caught up with him.

Nice going, B.A.S., old boy, I thought. You're doing fine. It isn't every skid-row pearl-diver who can reconstruct a crime out of nothing. Sheer genius, B.A.S., sheer genius.

But it was something to pass the

time, a lot better than staring at the wall and wishing I'd never left Chicago. Better than brooding.

All right, suppose it figured so far — then how did Mame's death tie in with it? I didn't see how. I made myself pace and concentrate, trying to work out an answer.

I felt sure Mame had been telling me the truth about Gonzales as far as she knew it, or else she would have had no reason for mentioning it at all. Whatever his ulterior motive in picking her up, whether to buy dope or to find a contact for selling it, he hadn't yet leveled with Mame before that knock came. Otherwise she wouldn't have told it casually, as she had, as something amusing.

But the killer wouldn't have known that. He couldn't have known that Mame was not an accomplice. If what he was looking for hadn't been on the person of the man he'd killed he could have figured that it had already changed hands. Why hadn't he gone back to Mame's the same night? I didn't know, but there could have been a reason. Perhaps he had and she'd gone out, locking the door and the fire escape window. Or maybe by that time she had other company; if he had knocked she might have opened the door on the chain — and I remembered now that there was a chain on her door — and told him so. I couldn't ask Mame now what she'd done the rest of the night after her jittery caller had left.

But if Gonzales was a stranger in town, just off the boat, how would the killer have known he had brought in heroin? — or opium or cocaine; it could have been any drug worth smuggling. And the killer must have known *something;* if it had been just a robbery kill, for whatever money Gonzales was carrying, then he wouldn't have gone back and killed Mame, searched her room. He'd have done that only if he'd known something about Gonzales that made him think Mame was his accomplice.

I killed a few more minutes worrying about that and I had the answer. Maybe not *the* answer, but at least an answer that made sense. Maybe I was just mildly cockeyed, but this off-the-cuff figuring I'd been doing *did* seem to be getting somewhere.

It was possible, I reasoned, that Mame hadn't been the first person through whom Gonzales had tried to make a contact. He could have approached another junkie on the same deal, but one who refused to tell him her contact. Her? It didn't have to be a woman, but Mame had been a woman and that made me think he'd been working that way. Say that he'd wandered around B-joints until he spotted a B-girl as an addict; he could get her in a booth and try to get information from her. She could have stalled him or turned him down. Stalled him, most likely, making a phone call or two to see if she could get hold of a dealer for him, but tipping off her boy friend instead. Killing time enough for her boy friend to be ready outside, then telling Gonzales she couldn't make a contact for him.

And if any of that had sounded suspicious to Gonzales he would have been more careful the second try, with Mame. He'd get her to her room on the obvious pretext, make sure they were alone and hadn't been followed before he opened up. Only, between The Best Chance and Mame's room, he must have discovered that they were being followed.

Sure, it all fitted. But what good did it do me?

Sure, it was logical. It made a complete and perfect picture, but it was all guesswork, nothing to go to the cops with. Even if they believed me eventually and could verify my guesses in the long run, I'd be getting myself and Billie the Kid into plenty of trouble in the short run. And like as not enough bad publicity — my relations with Billie would surely come out, and Billie's occupation — to have my father's clients in Chicago decide I wasn't fit to handle their business.

Well, was I? Worry about the fact that you want a drink so damned bad, I told myself, that soon you're going to weaken and go down and get another bottle. Well, why not? As long as I rationed it to myself so I would be drinking just enough to hold my own and not get drunk, not until after eight o'clock anyway . . .

What time was it? It seemed like I'd been in that damned room six or eight hours, but I'd checked in at around eleven and the sun was shining straight down in the dirty areaway my window opened on. Could it be only noon? I went out to the desk and past it, looking at the kitchen-type electric clock on the wall over it as I went by. It was a quarter after twelve.

I decided to walk a while before I went back to the room with a bottle, kill some time first. God, the time I had to kill before eight o'clock. I walked around the court house and over to Spring Street. I'd be safe there.

Hell, I'd be safe anywhere, I thought. Except maybe right in that one block of Fifth Street, just on the chance the police did have the milkman staked out in or near that building. And with different clothes, wearing a hat, he probably wouldn't recognize me anyway. Billie the Kid had panicked, and had panicked me. I didn't have anything to worry about. Oh, moving out of that block, changing out of the clothes I'd been wearing, those things had been sensible. But I didn't have to quit my job at Burke's — if it was still open to me. Burke's was safe for me. Nobody at Burke's knew where I'd lived and nobody in the building I'd lived in knew where I worked.

I thought, why not go to Burke's? He'd have the sign out in the window, now that I was an hour and a half late, but if nobody had taken the job, I could give him a story why I was so late and get it back. I'd gotten pretty good at washing dishes; I was probably the best dishwasher he'd ever had and I'd been steadier than the average one. Sure, I could go back there unless he'd managed to hire a new one already.

And otherwise, what? I'd either have to look for a new job of the same kind or keep on taking money from Billie for however long I stayed here. And taking money from Billie, except in emergency, was out. That gal named Honor back in Chicago was getting to be a pretty dim memory, but I still had some self-respect.

I cut back to Main Street and headed for Burke's. The back way, so I could see if anyone was working yet in my place, and maybe ask Ramon what the score was before I saw Burke.

From the alley doorway I could see my spot was empty, dishes piling high. Ramon was busy at the stove. He turned as I walked up to him, and his teeth flashed white in that grin. He said, "Howie! Thank God you're here. No dishwasher, everybody's going nuts."

The bandage was gone from his forehead. Under where it had been were four long scratches, downward, about an inch apart.

I stared at the scratches and thought about Ramon and his monkey and Mame and *her* monkey, and all of a sudden I had a crazy hunch. I thought about how a monkey like Ramon's could make a man do anything to get a fix. I moistened my lips. Ramon's monkey might claw the hell out of his guts, but it hadn't put those four scratches on his face. Not directly.

I didn't say it, I'd have had more sense; my mouth said it. "Mame had sharp fingernails, huh?"

5

Death can be a sudden thing. Only luck or accident kept me from dying suddenly in the next second or two. I'd never seen a face change as suddenly as Ramon's did. And before I could move, his hand had hold of the front of my shirt and his other hand had reached behind him and come up with and raised a cleaver. To step back as it started down would have put me in even better position for it to hit, so I did the only thing possible; I stepped in and pushed him backward and he stumbled and fell. I'd jerked my head but the cleaver went too wild even to scrape my shoulders. And there was a thunking sound as Ramon's head hit a sharp corner of the big stove. Yes, death can be a sudden thing.

I breathed hard a second and then — well, I don't know why I cared whether he was alive or not, but I bent forward and reached inside his shirt, held my hand over where his heart should be beating. It wasn't.

From the other side of the window Burke's voice sang out, "Two burgers, with."

I got out of there fast. Nobody had seen me there, nobody was *going* to see me there. I got out of the alley without being seen, that I knew of, and back to Main Street. I walked three blocks before I stopped into a tavern for the drink I really needed *now*. Not wine, whisky. Wine's an anodyne but it dulls the mind. Whisky sharpens it, at least temporarily. I ordered whisky, a double, straight.

I took half of it in one swallow and got over the worst of it. I sipped the rest slowly, and thought.

Damn it, Howie, I told myself, you've *got* to think.

I thought, and there was only one answer. I was in over my head now. If the police got me I was sunk. B.A.S. or not, I'd have a hell of a time convincing them I hadn't committed two murders — maybe three; if they'd tied in Jesus Gonzales, they'd pin that on me, too.

Sure, *I* knew what had really happened, but what proof did I have? Mame was dead; she wouldn't tell again what she'd told me about her little episode with Jesus. Ramon was dead; he wouldn't back up my otherwise unsupported word that I'd killed him accidentally in defending myself.

Out of this while I had a whole skin, that was the only answer. Back in Chicago, back to respectability, back to my right name — Howard Perry, B.A.S., not Howard Perry, bastard, wino, suspected soon of being a psychopathic killer. Back to Chicago, and not by freight. Too easy to get arrested that way, vagged, and maybe by that time flyers would be out with my description. Too risky.

So was waiting till eight o'clock when it was only one o'clock now. I'd have to risk getting in touch with Billie the Kid sooner. I couldn't go to her place, but I could phone. Surely they wouldn't have all the phones in that building tapped.

Just the same I was careful when I got her number. "Billie," I said, "this is the Professor." That nickname wouldn't mean anything to anybody else.

I heard her draw in her breath sharply. She must have realized I wouldn't risk calling her unless something important had come up. But she made her voice calm when she answered, "Yes, Professor?"

"Something has come up," I said. "I'm afraid I won't be able to make our eight o'clock date. Is there any chance that you can meet me now instead — same place?"

"Sure, soon as I can get there."

Click of the receiver. She'd be there. Billie the Kid, my Billie. She'd be there, and she'd make sure first that no one was following her. She'd bring money, knowing that I'd decided I had to lam after all. Money that she'd get back, damn it, if it was the last thing I ever did. Whatever money she'd lend me now, plus the other two sums and enough over to covet every drink and every cigarette I'd bummed from her. But not for the love and the trust she'd given me; you can't pay for that in money. In my case, I couldn't ever pay for it, period. The nearest I could come would be by being honest with her, leveling down the line. That much she had coming. More than that she had coming but more than that I couldn't give her.

The Shoebox is a shoebox-sized place. Not good for talking, but that didn't matter because we weren't going to talk there.

She got there fifteen minutes after I did; I was on my second drink. I ordered a Manhattan when I saw her coming in the door.

"Hello, Billie," I said.

Hello, Billie. Goodbye, Billie. This is the end for us, today. It's got to be the end. I knew she'd understand when I told her, when I told her everything.

"Howie, are you in —"

"In funds?" I cut her off. "Sure, just ordered you a drink." I dropped my voice, but not far enough to make it conspicuous. "Not here, Billie. Let's drink our drink and then I've got a room around the corner. I registered double so it'll be safe for us to go there and talk a while."

The bartender had mixed her Manhattan and was pouring it. I ordered a refill on my whisky-high. Why not? It was going to be my last drink for a long while. The wagon from here on in, even after I got back to Chicago for at least a few weeks, until I was sure the stuff couldn't get me, until I was sure I could do normal occasional social drinking without letting it start me off.

We drank our drinks and went out. Out into the sun, the warm sunny afternoon. Just before we got to the corner, Billie stopped me. "Just a minute, Howie."

She ducked into a store, a liquor store, before I could stop her. I waited. She came out with a wrapped bottle and a cardboard carton. "The ready-mixed wasn't on ice, Howie, but it's all right. I bought some ice cubes too. Are there two glasses in the room?"

I nodded; we went on. There were two glasses in the room. The wagon not yet. But it wouldn't have been right not to have a last drink or two, a stirrup cup or two, with Billie the Kid.

She took charge of the two tumblers, the drinks. Poured the drinks over ice cubes, stirred them around a while and then fished the ice cubes out when the drinks were chilled.

While I talked. While I told her about Chicago, about me in Chicago, about my family and the investment company. She handed me my drink then. She said quietly, "Go on, Howie."

I went on. I told her what Mame had told me about her guest Jesus the night before she was killed. I told her of the death of Jesus Gonzales as I'd read it in the *Mirror*. I added the two up for her.

She made us another drink while

I told her about Ramon, about what had happened, about how I'd just killed him.

"Ramon," she said. "He has knife scars, Howie?" I nodded. She said, "Knife scars, a hype, a chef. I didn't know his name, but I know who his woman was, a red-headed junkie named Bess, I think it's Bess, in a place just down the block from Karas' joint. It's what happened, Howie, just like you guessed it. It must have been." She sipped her drink. "Yes, Howie, you'd better go back to Chicago, right away. It could be bad trouble for you if you don't. I brought money. Sixty. It's all I have except a little to last me till I can get more. Here."

A little roll of bills, she tucked into my shirt pocket.

"Billie," I said. "I wish —"

"Don't say it, honey. I know you can't. Take me with you, I mean. I wouldn't fit, not with the people you know there. And I'd be bad for you."

"I'd be bad for you, Billie. I'd be a square, a wet blanket. I'll have to be to get back in that rut, to hold down —" I didn't want to think about it. I said, "Billie, I'm going to send you what I owe you. Can I count on your being at the same address for another week or so?"

She sighed. "I guess so, Howie. But I'll give you my sister's name and address, what I use for a permanent address, in case you ever — in case you might not be able to send the money right away."

"I'll write it down," I said. I tore a corner off the paper the bottle had been wrapped in, looked around for something to write with; I remembered the fountain pen I'd stuck in my trousers pocket at Mame's. It was still there.

I screwed off the cap. Something glittered, falling to the carpet, a lot of somethings. Shiny little somethings that looked like diamonds. Billie gasped. Then she was scrabbling on the floor, picking them up. I stared at the pen, the hollow pen without even a point, in my hand. Hollow and empty now. But there was still something in the cap, which I'd been holding so it hadn't spilled. I emptied the cap out into my hand. Bigger diamonds, six of them, big and deep and beautifully cut.

My guess had been wrong. It hadn't been heroin Gonzales had been smuggling. Diamonds. And when he'd found himself followed to Mame's, he'd stashed them there for safety: The pen hadn't fallen from his coat pocket; he'd hidden it there deliberately.

They were in two piles on the table, Billie's hands trembling a little as she handled them one at a time. "Matched," she said reverently. "My husband taught me stones, Howie. Those six big ones — over five carats each, cut for depth, not shallow, and they're blue-white and I'll bet they're flawless, all of them, because they're matched. And the fifteen smaller ones — they're matched too, and they're almost three carats apiece. You know what Karas would give us for them, Howie?"

"Karas?"

"Fifteen grand, Howie, at least. Maybe more. These aren't ordinary; they're something special. Sure, Karas — I didn't tell you everything, because it didn't matter then, when I said I thought maybe he had some racket — not dope. He handles stones, only stones. Gonzales might have heard of him, might have been trying to contact him through Mame."

I thought about fifteen thousand dollars, and I thought about going back to Chicago. Billie said, "Mexico, Howie. In Mexico we can live like kings — like a king and queen — for five years for that much."

And stop drinking, straighten out? Billie said, "Howie, shall I take these to Karas right now so we can leave quick?" She was flushed, breathing hard, staring at me pleadingly.

"Yes," I said. She kissed me, hard, and gathered them up.

At the doorway, hand on the knob. "Howie, were you kidding when you said you were in love with a girl named Honor in Chicago? I mean, is there a real girl named that, or did you just mean —?"

"I was kidding, Billie the Kid."

The door closed.

Her heels clicked down the wooden hall. I poured myself a drink, a long one, and didn't bother to chill it with ice cubes. Yes, I'd known a girl named Honor in Chicago, once, but — . . . *but that was in another country, and besides, the wench is dead.*

I drank my drink and waited.

Twenty minutes later, I heard Billie's returning footsteps in the hall.

Quiet Day in the County Jail

"She was so beautiful and so pale,
She seemed so young, too fair to die
As she sat on her cot in the jail
With a tear in her lovely eye ——"

"CUT that singing out, Artie," the girl's voice called.

Artie, the head trusty, put down his guitar and walked into the cell that was half of what had been named the Presidential Suite. It

They all kept assuring her she'd be perfectly safe, but they knew the chances were she was going to be murdered.

BY CRAIG RICE

was unlocked, because its tenant was only being held in protective custody as a material witness.

"What's the matter, Red?" he asked gently. "You nervous?"

She was beautiful, and she was pale, and she did seem too young and too fair to die. She was sitting on the edge of her bunk, wrapped in a green chenille bathrobe. The hair that had given her her nickname was loose over her shoulders. A cigarette blazed between her trembling fingers.

"Shadow fell over my tombstone, I guess," she said. "Forget it."

He patted her awkwardly on the shoulder and said "You'd better get some sleep while you can." Right away he knew that had been the wrong thing to say, but it was too late to do anything about it now.

She looked at him with eyes that, for a moment, were bright with fear. "You don't need to remind me. They can't let me get back to Detroit alive."

"Shut up, Red," he said, even more gently. "That isn't what I meant." His voice managed to get back to normal. "I mean they're bringing in Aggie."

"Hot damn!" A smile and a little color came back to her face. "Well," she said thoughtfully," the jail does need a good cleaning." She crushed out her cigarette in the fruit jar top that served as an ash-tray. "Artie, is there a drink anywhere in the house?"

"Need one?" He looked at her, a mixture of admiration, brotherly affection, sympathy, and a touch of fear. "We confiscated a pint of gin off a guy. Most of it's left. I'll get it."

Her lower lip was trembling almost as much as her pale fingers.

"Red, kid," he said softly, "you're in the safest place in the world. Jail, that is. Everything is going to be all right."

He grinned at her reassuringly, paused at the door, and burst into song again.

"*The sheriff spoke in a quiet tone,*
She seemed so beautiful and so young,
As he said, 'tonight you're all alone,
'And tomorrow you must be hung ——' "

He ducked the folded magazine she threw at him and said "Take it easy, Red. Even the President doesn't have a better bodyguard. I'll be right back."

The Santa Maria County Jail was as informal as a Sunday School picnic, and on weekends and holidays, twice as noisy. Small, and fitted with only the essentials, it filled the second floor of the police station. The Presidential Suite consisted of two cells in a far corner, reserved for women, juveniles, and special prisoners. Right now, Red had it to herself.

Because she wasn't, strictly speaking, a prisoner, and because she had her bankroll with her, the cell had sheets, a pillow and pillow case. Her expensive clothes were carefully placed on hangers. And because Red was a friendly person, a bunch of blue flowers smiled from a jelly glass on an improvised table that had been made of two suitcases and a length of board.

Artie came back, his hand under his tan jacket. The cell was in semi-darkness, Red was still sitting on the edge of the bunk. He picked up the white enameled cup from the wash-stand, poured in a generous drink, added a little water, and handed it to her.

"Dirty trick," Red said. "Toss a guy in the can, and then take his gin away."

"He won't miss it," Artie assured her. "He's the Mayor's second cousin, and he's got eighteen dollars on deposit downstairs." He added, "You'd better keep the bottle."

"I may need it," she said. She looked up at him, six foot if he was half an inch, crew cut blond hair, a deeply lined face. She slid the bottle between the mattresses of the bunk across from her, downed the contents of the cup fast, choked, and gasped, "*Water!*"

Artie rushed it to her. "Next time, hold your breath." He paused. "Red, you aren't really scared, are you?"

"Who, me?" she said, turning her eyes away. Her hands shook as she gulped the water, and half of it spilled on the floor.

"Red, kid," he said, taking the cup from her hands. "All you got to do is wait till they take you back to Detroit, just for you to testify. Then you're in the clear."

"They'll never let me get to that courtroom," she said, very quietly.

"Don't talk silly," Artie said. "You'll be protected. You'll be safe."

Their eyes met. They were both lying, and they both knew it.

She turned away first, punched up her pillow, lit a cigarette and said, "Let's talk about you. What happens? I saw your lawyer come up here yesterday."

"The case comes up week after next," Artie said. "If the judge gets well, that is. The county's only got two judges, and one of 'em's sick. Two thousand cases were ahead of me, but they got it down to one thousand nine hundred and forty-four. When this other judge gets over his tonsillitis, or ulcers, or beri-beri, or whatever it is, I'm first on the calendar. It'll be a short trial. They reduced the charge to man-slaughter, and my lawyer's charging self-defense."

He blew his nose, lit a cigarette. "Red," he said, "I love my wife. She wrote me every day I was in the South Pacific. I love my kids. She brings them to see me every Sunday. I have a nice little ranch, I'm building up a trucking business. I met this guy, he came over to my house, the wife and kids were up visiting her mother, we had a few beers. He went wild and pulled a gun on me. I tried to take it away from him, and it went off."

Red reached between the mattresses for the bottle, poured a generous two inches into the cup and handed it to Artie. She had a hunch it was he who needed moral support now.

"You'll get off," she told him. "They may even give you a bounty."

That got a laugh out of him, which was what she wanted. He flicked the ash from his cigarette and said "Hell, it hasn't been too bad here, these eleven months. Since I been a trusty, I got the run of the place. I go out and do marketing, run errands, eat good and sleep good. Could be worse."

She said with a tired quietness, "I'd rather be here than dead in the streets."

"Red, you quit that kind of talk."

"They got to get me before I can testify," she said.

"I told you before, you're in the safest place in the world."

Suddenly the jail seemed to shake. There were sounds from downstairs, just a little louder than the Bronx Zoo at feeding time, and at about the same pitch.

"That would be Aggie," Red said.

"Couldn't be anyone else." Artie grinned. He rose, locked her cell door and said "Sorry I have to do this, but it's only for a few minutes. He called "Hey, Pablo!"

Red settled down on her bunk and listened to the rumpus. Aggie was resisting arrest in two languages, and from the sounds, it was taking both trusties and Fred, the night jailer, to hold her.

Aggie was probably the best cleaning woman in Santa Maria. She was also probably the loudest drunk. She was happy with a bottle, she was just as happy with a pail of soap and water and a mop. Periodically when the jail needed a thorough scrubbing, the word went down the line "Tour the bars and pick up Aggie."

Aggie always was brought into the jail sounding like a combination of a major riot and a bomb landing in the next block. Next morning the judge invariably sentenced her to six days, which could be worked out in three, and Aggie, cheerful if slightly hung over, filled a pail with soap and hot water and reached for the nearest mop.

Red put her fingers in her ears as Aggie was shoved into the next door cell and locked in. Aggie went right on shouting.

Artie unlocked the metal grill door to Red's room and said "You asleep?"

"Slept right through it," Red said cheerfully.

The other trusty, the small, sad-eyed Pablo, came in with Artie. "This we take from Aggie," he said gravely.

The bottle was passed around solemnly. Red shuddered. "Can't these cops ever arrest anybody with champagne?"

"Me, I like scotch," Artie said.

She passed the bottle to him. "Shut your eyes and pretend that it's scotch."

There was more noise from the cell next door.

"That Aggie, she makes with the yell," Pablo said.

"I make with the yell myself," Red said grimly. She raised her voice. "Shut up!"

There was a moment's silence, and then an answering yell. "You're who, and what'cha here for?"

"I'm the axe killer you been reading about in the papers," Red called. "And I've got the axe right here, the one I chopped up seven people with. The police let me keep it because I know the Mayor. And my cell door is unlocked, and I've got a key to yours, and I like it quiet when I sleep."

There was a long, and what promised to be, a night long silence.

Artie and Pablo waved goodnight and went away.

That was at four a.m.

By eight o'clock in the morning, the sun had been turning the heat on for an hour and a half. Red stirred restlessly, felt a hand pat her shoulder gently, turned over and opened her eyes.

It was Fred, the night jailer. "Going off duty now, Red. Just came by to say goodbye and wish you luck."

Suddenly wide awake, she sat up, pulling the blankets around her shoulders. "What do you mean, goodbye?"

Fred looked embarrassed. "I thought they were moving you out today."

"Nobody's told me yet," she said. She didn't need to look in a mirror, she could feel her face turning pale.

"Well," he said, "well, in case they do. Good luck. Don't worry, Red. Come back and visit us when it's all over."

"Sure will," she said heartily. "I'll do just that little thing."

He knew she'd never be back in Santa Maria, and so did she.

They shook hands. She said, "Fred, please thank your wife for sending me the flowers." Flowers for a corpse that was still walking around and talking. "Wait a minute, will you."

She reached for her robe, wrapped it around her, slid off the bunk and rummaged through the suitcase that was under the bed, until she pulled out what looked like a handful of tissue paper. She sat on the edge of the bunk, untangled the tissue paper, and pulled out a brooch. It blazed green, yellow and white fire in the early morning sunlight.

"Please give this to her. It's a phony, just a hunk of costume jewelry, but I think it's pretty. The one thing that isn't phony is the thanks to her that go with it."

"Gosh, Red," Fred said. He choked for a minute, rewrapped the brooch in the tissue paper, and stuck it in his pocket. "Gosh." He paused again. "She wanted to send you some more flowers."

"Tell her to save them for my wake," Red said, managing to keep her voice light. She walked over to the window and stood looking out.

Fred stood for a moment, uncertainty drawn on his broad red face. Finally he walked over and put a hand on her arm. "Red," he said, feeling for words, "if — I mean, if something happens to you — I mean, well, I got friends, we'll find out who did it —"

She turned around, smiling. "Thanks. Now beat it, bum. I've got to get some sleep."

There was something she vaguely remembered from High School. She fished for it in her mind, and all that came to her was "There is a time to sleep, and a time to stay awake." She knew that wasn't right, but it didn't matter now.

She paced up and down the cell. She scrubbed her face and put on fresh make-up. She combed her lovely red hair until it was smooth and shining. She brushed on lipstick and tended to her eyebrows. She put on a pair of dove-grey slacks, a pale green sweater, and darker green sandals.

Eight thirty. She remembered Aggie with a sudden sense of guilt. She raced into the main room and yelled for Artie.

"Honey, open up Aggie's door. She's got to be in court by nine, and I've got to wash her face."

"Will do," he said, reaching for the keys. He looked appreciatively. "You're going to be missed, Red."

Again she could feel the color drain out of her face. "Who says?"

Artie avoided her eyes as he unlocked the door to Aggie's cell. After a moment of inspection and thought, Red went next door and collected a comb, make-up, powder, a lipstick, a big fluffy towel, mouthwash, and the remains of the gin. Five vigorous shakes woke Aggie.

"Come on, kid," Red said. "You've got to be in court in half an hour."

Aggie began moaning. An inch of gin in the enameled cup took care of that. She got her eyes open enough to stay that way on the fourth blink, and said "Red! You still here?"

"Haven't thrown me out yet," Red said, with false cheerfulness. "Babe, do yourself proud in court. Wash your face, and I'll put your make-up on for you, and fix your hair." She looked at Aggie's dress and shook her head sadly.

Well, there was one of her own that just might fit. She was as tall as Aggie, and the dress would stretch sideways.

At two minutes to nine, Aggie was on her way downstairs, hair combed, face made up, smelling slightly of mouthwash and Daphne Cologne, and wearing a blue jersey dress that would never shrink back into shape again.

At ten minutes after nine, Aggie came back up the stairs, beaming. "Six or three," she shouted. "Artie, where's the mop?"

Red called from her cell "Artie! Pablo! Somebody!"

It was Artie who came to the door. "A mouse?" he asked.

"I want breakfast," Red said.

"Breakfast is served in this jail at six thirty," Artie said. "But since you slipped Frank a buck yesterday to buy eggs, I think we can oblige you." He winked at her. "He got a dozen eggs stashed away in the refrigerator. And the coffee's good this morning."

It was Pablo who brought in the tin tray. The eggs were cooked just right, the toast was the right color of tan, and the coffee was as good as advertised.

She smiled at Pablo. She always smiled at Pablo. Today she had an extra one.

Pablo was short and slender and black-haired, and he was almost a permanent prisoner. Frank, the day jailer, had confided in Red that Pablo had been serving a thirty-day drunk charge for almost two years. It had become a regular routine. Sentenced to thirty days. Made a trusty the next day. Released. Arrested the next day, or even sooner.

Artie swore, and Red believed him, that Pablo had once made the round trip from the jail and back in exactly three hours.

And it was Artie who'd told her how Pablo's wife had run away with another man, how he'd lost his job, and seen the bank take away his home, all in one month.

"Senorita Red," Pablo said, "would you like I should go and buy you cigarettes?"

She looked at him with pretended sternness. "The last time I gave you a quarter to buy me cigarettes you were gone for two days, and the judge tacked an extra thirty days on you when they did find you."

"It was a mistake," Pablo said with great dignity. "Perhaps you could lend me twenty-five cents. Believe me, it is for a good purpose."

She looked at him and her eyes softened. After all, Pablo had only two homes. The jail, and the Frisco Bar and Grill. She pulled her change purse from under her pillow, took out a fifty cent piece, and said "I hope you have a lot of fun with the good purpose."

That was at ten o'clock in the morning.

The routine daily cleaning was going on, plus Aggie throwing a mop around in the kitchen. Red stood looking out the window at the roof of the bowling alley next door. She lifted her eyes to the mountains that ringed the little city and saw a tiny speck of silver racing across the blue. Would they take her out by plane, or train, she wondered.

She could hear Artie going through the big cabinet in the main room, sorting out files. She could hear a prisoner rattling tin trays in the kitchen sink. This will be going on long after I'm gone, she thought. Artie will go on sorting files, then his case will come up in court and chances are he'll be freed; the guy in the kitchen will go on washing dishes and serve his sentence and be on his way. But she would be gone before that, far away from here.

A voice said "Hey, Red."

She turned around. It was Frank, the day jailer. He was a deceptively gentle-looking man with a friendly face, white hair, and a deadly right when he had to use it. He was one more person in the world she would have trusted with her life.

"Chief's on his way up to see you. Thought I'd tell you, case you want to powder your face."

"Bless you, Frank." At that moment she heard the buzzer that announced someone was coming up the stairs.

She was sitting on the edge of her bunk, face powdered, when Chief of Police Sankey came in, Frank close behind him.

"Red," he said. "I mean, Miss —"

"That's all right," she said.

He sat down on the bunk across from her, a worried, fretful little man with reddish hair and rimless glasses.

"Well," he said, "we finally got the word. They're taking you on a plane this afternoon. Papers all signed, everything set."

She opened her mouth to speak, shut it again, and finally managed to say "I'll be ready."

He looked embarrassed. He said "You'll be well protected, naturally. So there's nothing for you to worry about." He paused and added "Well, good luck."

After he'd gone, Frank patted her shoulder and said "Everything's going to be all right, Red."

"Oh, sure." She forced a smile to her face. "It's just that I like your jail so well that I hate to leave it. Besides, I feel safe here."

He cleared his throat, started to speak and changed his mind. He patted her shoulder a second time.

"Frank, I saw the whole thing. I was standing right in the doorway of the Blue Casino. Louie did the job himself, and I was right there. All I could think of was to beat it, fast. Threw some stuff in a couple of suitcases, got the first plane to Kansas City. That's where I bought the car and headed south. I could have made it across the border into Mexico easy, but you guys picked me up."

"Maybe it's just as well," Frank told her reassuringly. "This guy would have had you followed. This way he'll get convicted, and then you won't have a thing to worry about."

"Oh, sure," she said again. She sighed. "It's just luck that some goon was coming down the sidewalk and saw what was going on. He didn't get close enough to recognize Louie, but I was standing there with a light smack on my face, and he spotted me. The Detroit cops picked up Louie on general principles and started looking for me."

She ran a hand through her

shining red hair. "I'm their only witness. 'Course, I could get on the stand and swear I didn't see a thing, or I could swear it wasn't Louie."

"You could," Frank said. "But —"

"But I wouldn't," she finished for him. "That is, assuming I ever get to the witness stand."

Artie came in, lit a cigarette, and lounged against the wall.

"This Louie," Frank asked, "was he your boyfriend?"

That brought a laugh from her, the first one that day. "I didn't have a boyfriend. I ran the Blue Casino. A gambling joint. I ran that end of it, and my partner ran the night club end." She grinned at them. "I came by these diamonds honestly, pals."

"So that's why you've been able to take us at blackjack," Artie said lazily.

"Well," Frank said, getting up, "you'll be protected on the way to the plane, and you'll be protected on the plane, and you'll probably be taken off it in an armored car."

Artie pinched out his cigarette, dropped it on the floor. "Pablo'll clean up in here when he gets back. He's got the car out now, getting potatoes."

At that moment, all hell broke loose in the yard outside. Red and Artie were tied getting to the window. Artie gave a loud whoop and raced for the stairs, yelling for Frank to work the buzzer.

Outside, Pablo was having troubles. The car used by the jail for general errands was parked directly under Red's window, and the trunk compartment was open. What appeared to be about a hundred white chickens, but were actually only six, were creating the disturbance. Pablo was trying to move them from the trunk compartment to a burlap bag, and the chickens were resisting arrest. The scene was beginning to draw a fair-sized audience when reinforcements, in the person of Artie, arrived.

Between them, the chickens were shoved unceremoniously into the bag and tossed, still protesting loudly, in the car. Artie and Pablo got in and drove off.

Frank, who had watched the last act from Red's window, sighed deeply and said "Sometimes I think they give these trusties too many liberties."

"None of them give you any trouble, though," Red reminded him.

"That's right," he said, "except sometimes Pablo." He looked at her searchingly. "Did you give him any money?"

"I gave him fifty cents," Red confessed. She added as though in defense, "After all, Frank, it's my last day here."

Frank shook his head sadly. "Another thirty days. Well, he's got to sleep somewhere."

That was at eleven o'clock.

It was sometime later when Artie and Pablo came in triumphantly,

Pablo carrying a large paper-wrapped bundle. The chickens were not only silent now, but in addition to losing their voices, they had lost their feathers and a few other odds and ends, and were candidates for the frying pan.

"Farewell party!" Artie called happily, heading for the kitchen.

Red looked at her suitcases, at the clothes hanging against the walls, at the make-up carefully arranged on the improvised table, and started a half-hearted effort toward packing. But there was plenty of time for that later. She flopped down on the bunk, picked up a magazine and tried to read. The words seemed to run together and made no sense at all.

Pablo came in the door. He was completely sober, and walking with great dignity. He carried a package which he presented to Red with even greater dignity.

"For you," he said. "For a going-far-away present."

She unwrapped it. It was a bottle of what was probably the worst wine in the world. This was the important purpose for which Pablo had needed money. She felt tears hot in her eyes.

"Pablo, I thank you," she said with dignity that matched his. She put the package under the bunk, reached between the mattresses for the last of the gin. "For farewell, will you have a drink with me?"

Pablo's dark eyes brightened. "Since you insist upon it."

She rinsed out the enameled cups and divided the gin equally into them. They saluted each other solemnly and silently.

"We will miss you," Pablo said simply.

That was at twelve o'clock.

It was Artie who brought in her lunch, sometime later.

"No stew?" she said, looking up and sniffing. "No pinto beans?"

Artie grinned at her as he set the tray down. "Fried chicken." He shook his head thoughtfully. "That Pablo. It isn't enough that he goes out and steals chickens. But he has to steal the chickens from the Chief of Police."

He went on. "He was going to bring them up here and clean them, but I had an idea. We took them to a restaurant where I know the kitchen help. Result, no evidence."

It was one o'clock when he came to take the tray away, and lock Aggie's door. She was, after all, a prisoner, and even in the Santa Maria County Jail, rules were rules. He paused in Red's cell.

"I'll help you pack, after siesta."

She turned her face away. "I can manage, thanks, Artie."

He sat down on the other bunk. "Red, listen. You'll be protected. There's nothing to it. When you get to Detroit they'll put you up in some expensive hotel, with a body-guard. You testify, and it's all over. There's nothing for you to be scared."

"Who's scared?" she scoffed, managing to keep her voice steady.

"Red," he said slowly, "Red. Will you let me kiss you, once?"

She stared at him.

"I been here eleven months, Red. I'd just like to kiss a girl again."

She smiled, and lifted her face to him. He kissed her very gently, almost a little boy kiss.

"It won't seem like the same place without you, Red."

The county jail became silent. Frank had gone out to lunch and everyone else was asleep. Everybody except Red. She lay on her bunk, her eyes closed, wondering if she would ever sleep again. Finally, she gave up. Might as well pack and get it over with.

Mid-afternoon sunlight was streaming in the windows of the trusties' room when the sound of the big door clanging shut and footsteps on the stairs woke Artie. He swung his long legs off the bed, and walked into the main room.

That was at three o'clock.

Frank and a stranger had just reached the top of the stairs.

"Detective Connelly, Detroit police," Frank said, puffing, and nodding toward the stranger. "Red all packed and set to leave?"

"I'll see," Artie said.

Red was sitting on the bunk, her suitcase beside her. She had on a light beige suit and a small green hat. Her face was very pale. Artie picked up the suitcase. She rose and followed him into the main room.

Pablo had come out of the trusties' room. Aggie, mop in hand, was watching. Everyone was silent.

Red managed a wan smile at the Detroit detective.

"All set?" He tried to smile but didn't look as though he relished this job. She nodded.

Frank said heartily, "Now remember, Red, don't you worry about a thing. He'll take you back, you testify, this Louie will go to jail or the chair, and that's that."

"Sure," Connelly said, with false confidence. "That's the way."

"And you will come back to visit us," Pablo said. "I will still be here."

That eased the tension a little.

There was nothing left to say but goodbye. Then Red went down the stairs without looking back, Connelly and Frank on either side. The two trusties stood looking after her.

At last they walked to her cell and looked in. There was a faint odor of cigarette smoke, gin, and expensive perfume. Artie straightened a wrinkle in the blankets.

"It seems so quiet," he said.

Pablo looked under the bed, pulled out the package. "She forgets and leaves it behind," he said sadly, unwrapping it. "I buy it for her, a going away present." There were tears in his eyes.

"You're a bad boy, Pablo," Aggie said from the doorway.

Pablo looked wistfully.

"I think she'd have wanted you to open it," Artie said, very gently.

Pablo ripped off the cap. The bottle of the worst wine in the world was passed around in silence.

I'll Kill for You

BY

FLETCHER FLORA

Caldwell was dead, and Frost knew who killed him. The trouble was — the girl knew, too.

SHE got out of the yellow cab in front of the apartment building and stood for a few seconds at the curb as she searched her purse for the fare. I stood at the corner beside a public trash can and watched her until she had paid the cabby and crossed the sidewalk. Her spike heels rapped out a brisk tattoo on concrete. The pneumatic catch on the apartment door gave a sharp gasp, trailing off into a long, expiring sigh.

I waited until the cab had whisked its red tail light around the far corner, then I went down to the entrance and in after her. Behind me, the door gasped and sighed again. It was a sad sound. A lost and damned sound. It was like a last whimper of regret at the doorway to hell.

Inside, the lobby was empty. From the elevator well came the soft, pervasive whine of the ascending car. I went across the lobby quickly and stood watching the arrow of the floor indicator move around to six. It stopped there, not quite half way around the circumference of the dial, and above me, echoing with hollow faintness down the deep shaft, was the distant sound of doors opening and closing.

Turning away, walking fast, I started up the stairs, taking them two at a time, but not running. The stairs were wide, about eight feet, for the first two flights. Above that, they narrowed to four and continued upward in an economy of light. On each landing, where the angle of ascension turned back on itself, there was a single red bulb. When I passed under the bulbs, my abbreviated shadow leaped ahead of me with startling suddenness, dying in shadow as abruptly.

I paced myself, two steps to a stride, until I came up off the stairs into the sixth floor hall. I stood there at the head of the flight, one hand on the steel post of the railing, and listened to the echo of my heart in my brain. It was a kind of accelerated tom-tom beat that was not arhythmic but was much too fast. I waited until the cadence subsided, and then I walked down the hall to a door that bore on its bleached surface the arabic identification six-o-three in chaste chrome.

The knob of the door turned under the pressure of my fingers, releasing the catch without sound, and I stood motionless for maybe three minutes, palming the knob and listening. There was no sound within the room. Cracking the door enough for passage, I slipped through into a small vestibule and pushed the door shut behind me. The catch slipped into position with the tiniest of oiled clicks. Moving swiftly, I took three long strides to the entrance to the living room and looked in.

She was standing almost in the middle of the room, just at the end of the sofa, with her back to me. Even from a distance, I could see that her muscles were as stiff as wood, that her flesh, to the touch, would be as cold as ice. She stood with her head bent forward and her eyes focused on the floor beyond the sofa, the light gleaming on the pale, silken cascade of her hair.

I stirred, made a sound, and she whipped around with a shrill intake of breath that tore at her constricted throat and must have hurt like the hacking of a dull blade. Her eyes flared in her drawn face, and scarlet lips that were all paint and no blood opened on the shape of a projected scream. But the scream never materialized. Closing in on her, I slashed my open hand across her cheek with a flat smack. She swayed, choking on the scream with a little animal whimper, but her feet didn't move on the carpet. The marks of four fingers were livid on her flesh.

"Don't," I said. "Don't scream."

She stared at me with her eyes wide and dry and hot and the marks of my fingers like a brand on her face. She didn't speak or make another sound until her breasts rose finally on a deep, ragged breath that held them for a long moment high and tight against the thin stuff of her dress. They descended on a long, controlled exhalation. I knew then that there was no more danger of hysteria, and I moved around her and beyond the sofa and stood looking down at the body on the carpet.

He lay sprawled on his face with

one arm stretched out beyond his head with the fingers clawed, as if in the last instant he had been clutching for the light that had escaped his brain through a matted mass of hair and blood and bone and soft gray matter. Beyond the reaching fingers, lying on its side in the thick pile of the carpet, was a highball glass. A wet stain spread out from the lip of the glass, and in the stain there were still two tiny fragments of melting ice cubes.

"A good, thorough job," I said, hearing behind me the soft hiss of her breath as the brutal remark slugged home.

Turning back to her, I saw that blood had returned to modify the livid smear of paint on her lips. Feverish stains were spread under the taut skin over the high bones of her cheeks.

"Why?" I said.

"Why?" She repeated the word on a suction, giving it shrill, rising inflection.

I gestured downward at the sprawled body. "Why did you kill him?"

"Kill him? Me?" Comprehension seemed to filter into. her mind slowly, in a slow seepage, as water soaks through the pores of old brick.

I shrugged angrily, and my voice sounded loud, needlessly harsh, in my own ears. "Look, honey. He's dead. He's lying there with the back of his head blown off. I come in and find you standing over him, and his bourbon not even dry on the floor where he spilled it. What the hell am I supposed to think?"

"I didn't kill him. I loved him. I would never have killed him."

"Loving and killing aren't incompatible. Sometimes, under the right circumstances, killing is a natural development. It's happened more times than you or I could count."

Her hot eyes seemed to cloud with confusion, as if her mind were groping dumbly for a convincer, and then they cleared suddenly, acquiring a glittering intentness.

"Where's the gun?"

The question was like a short jab to the solar plexus. I stood very still, not breathing, watching in her face the slow signs of returning assurance. After a few seconds, I dropped to my knees and looked under the sofa. Getting up, I prowled the room, looking in all the places a gun might have been dropped or thrown or placed. When I'd worked back to her, she hadn't moved. Her eyes, still hot and dry, had completely lost their dilation, shining now with that bright intentness. Her lips were parted, fluttering very slightly with the passage of long, deep breaths. The tip of her pink tongue flicked out and around them. Reaching out, I separated her stiff fingers from the suede purse they were clutching. I rummaged for a minute and gave it back.

"Okay," I said. "No gun. The killer must have taken it away."

She said abruptly, "What are you doing here?" Her voice broke.

I shrugged, looking into her dry, fever-infested eyes. "What's the difference? It makes no difference now."

"Maybe not. Unless you've been here before."

I laughed harshly. "To kill him, you mean? So then I come right back and show myself. Don't be a fool, honey."

Her head jerked around under a sudden strong compulsion, and her eyes dropped again to the husk on the floor. She may have experienced, in that instant, an intense sensory recollection of the look and smell and feel of him in the neural and glandular riot of the passion they had shared. However it was, when she turned back to me her eyes had lost their bright wariness and were filled instead with an incredible, flaring anguish.

I felt, all at once, very tired. "You'd better get out of here," I said. "You'd better get the hell home in a hurry."

"What about you?"

I turned my back and fumbled in my coat for cigarettes. The smoke of the tobacco was caustic in my lungs, leaving an acrid taste on my tongue.

"There's a dead man on the floor, honey. Someone killed him. It adds up to cops. When you leave, I'll call them."

I stood there with my back to her, and for quite a while there was no sound at all. Then there was the silken rustle of movement and, from a long, long way off, maybe the distance to the end of everything, the faint, oily click of the door catch. My ear drums picked up the sound and amplified it, rolling it around the interior of my skull like the thunder of artillery around a rim of enclosing hills.

The telephone was on a table beyond the body. The outstretched arm seemed to be pointing to it, showing the way like a sign on a map. Making a careful detour, I went over and called the police.

"I want to report a murder," I said.

I waited until the call was channeled to Homicide and a tired voice came on. We went through a weary routine of question and answer.

Name?

Address?

Sit tight and don't touch anything.

I cradled the phone and went out into the kitchen.

In the kitchen, I sat on a tall stool and lit another cigarette. The faucet was dripping in the sink. I figured that it took about three seconds for a drop of water to form on the lip of the faucet and fall off into the sink. The drops struck the porcelain with almost mathematical regularity, making small tapping sounds. Tap . . . tap . . . tap. I started to count the sounds of the drops striking the porcelain, and I had counted four hundred and six when there was movement in the living room. I got off the stool and went in.

A medium-sized guy in a loose brown suit was standing just inside the vestibule. His eyes toured me as I came through the door, moving off to a point of focus on the wall, as if they'd had all they wanted in short order. He had a narrow face with a long hooked nose and flesh that sagged from the bones. His voice was resigned, characterized by a heavy patience that remained as a habit even when it wasn't appropriate.

"Your name Henry Frost?"

"That's right."

"You call Homicide?"

"Yes."

"I'm it. Dunn's the name. Detective-Lieutenant."

Maybe I was supposed to make like a host. Maybe I was supposed to smile and be amiable. His eyes crossed me again to another point o focus, and he waited with that heavy patience and gave me no help whatever.

"The body's this side of the sofa," I said.

He moved to the sofa with a kind of easy shuffle and looked over the back. "So it is," he said.

Behind him, another man materialized from the vestibule and leaned against the jamb. He had something in his teeth and was working at it with a wooden match. He didn't bother to look at me at all.

"Who is he?" Dunn said.

"His name was Caldwell. Bruce Caldwell."

"Who's been here with you?" He stabbed a finger at the body. "Besides him, I mean."

"No one."

"You wearing perfume?"

"Do I look like the kind of man who'd wear perfume, for God's sake?"

His eyes smeared me again with their weary patience. "I don't know. I don't know what a man who'd wear perfume is supposed to look like. As far as I'm concerned, you look like a man who'd do anything, even murder. No offense. That's just a way of saying you look a hell of a lot like every other man I've ever seen." He stabbed again with the finger. "I wonder if he's wearing it."

"I wouldn't be surprised."

His eyebrows arched hairy backs. "That supposed to mean something?"

"You might figure it to mean something."

"Lover-boy, you mean? Hot number with the dames?"

"Something like that."

"You married?"

"Yes."

"I wonder if I could figure *that* to mean something?"

"You could try, but you're wasting your time."

He shrugged and a ragged little sound that might have been a chuckle came out of his throat. "Hell, I'm wasting time right now." He moved around the sofa, the thin edges of his nostrils quivering. "You smell the perfume? Don't you?"

I smelled it, all right. A delicate astringency suspended in cordite. It made me sick.

"Yes," I said.

"You know any dame who wears perfume that smells like that?"

"I can't think of any. It's probably a common scent."

"Sure. Probably. It may have been a dame who got him. If he was the kind of guy you imply, a dame's a good bet." He stopped and looked up at me again, and his lips curved in a gentle smile. "Or a husband," he said.

Kneeling beside the body, he got a handful of hair and lifted the head, looking in at an angle at the exposed profile. When he stood up, his hand was bloody. Taking a white handkerchief from his hip pocket, he wiped the hand carefully.

"Pretty," he said. "Real pretty. Lay him in a casket so the back of his head doesn't show, he'll be a real tear-jerker for those dames you mentioned. Well, we got work to do. You go on back in the kitchen and wait around. I'll talk to you some more later."

I went back into the kitchen and crawled onto the stool again. I heard more men come into the living room from the hall. They moved around, talking, and after a while I heard the explosion of flash-bulbs and caught the acrid odor of powder.

I could also hear the faucet dripping. I started counting the small sounds again, and the higher I counted the louder the sounds got, until finally each drip was like the detonation of a grenade inside my skull. I quit counting then and tried to ignore the drips, but by that time it was impossible, and the grenades kept right on detonating in my head. It was like the old Chinese torture chestnut, and I was about to go out and tell Dunn that I had to get the hell out of there when he came in, instead.

He pulled himself up onto the edge of the cabinet beside the sink and peered at me through a thin, drifting plume of smoke.

"I guess we're about finished in there," he said. "We didn't find much of anything that looks like it would be any help. Way I got it figured, he had someone with him, and they were having a drink. A guy named Henry Frost, say. Just to give him a name, you understand. It simplifies talking about him if he's got a name."

"I thought you'd settled for a woman," I said.

He smiled his gentle smile and looked at me through the pale blue, transparent plume. "Anyhow," he went on, "the phone rang. This guy Caldwell turned around with his glass in his hand to go to the phone, and that's when he was killed."

I felt as if someone had reached inside me and grabbed a handful of entrails. "How do you know that?" I said.

"I got the idea from the way he was lying. Like he'd been heading for the phone, you know. It figures, too. Once Caldwell got on the phone, it might have been too late for murder. Because he might just mention that Frost was there, and that would never do. You know how these phone conversations go. 'Busy, Caldwell?' 'Not particularly. Just having a drink with Henry Frost.' You see what I mean? Once he said that, there couldn't be any murder. I'll check to see if there was a call through the switchboard."

"I wish you wouldn't use my name," I said.

His mirthless chuckle came up again behind the gentle smile. "You shouldn't be so sensitive. Like I said, it's just a convenience. How come you came here tonight?"

"I had an appointment."

"Oh?"

"I'm a lawyer. Caldwell wanted to see me."

"So that's it. I guess a guy like Caldwell needed a lawyer pretty often. You ever handle anything for him before?"

"No."

"Don't you have an office? You make a practice of calling on clients to do business?"

"I don't make a practice. Sometimes I make an exception."

"Well, that's a fast answer. I can see you're a lawyer, all right. What was it about?"

"Why he wanted to see me? I don't know. He was dead when I got here."

"Sure. DOA. He never put out any hints earlier?"

"None whatever," I replied.

"Okay. What's your address?"

I told him, and he wrote it down in a little book. He wrote it very slowly, in tiny characters, with the stub of a pencil. He read it back, and I said it was right, and he put the book and the pencil in the breast pocket of his coat.

"You can go now," he said. "Later we'll want you to make a formal statement and sign it. By that time, I may have thought of something else to ask you."

I said all right and good-night and went out through the living room. The guy who'd come in with Dunn was sitting on the sofa with his feet up. Everyone else was gone, and some of those who'd come and gone had taken Bruce Caldwell with them. I went out into the hall and down in the elevator and outside.

A police car was standing by the curb. A cool wind was blowing down the deep canyon of the street, and I could see, looking up beyond the faint flush of city lights, the cold and distant stars.

I'd parked my car on a side street. I walked down to the corner and around it and stopped in the shadow of the building. I stood quietly for a moment with my shoulders braced against brick, then I moved to the corner of the building and looked back at the police car. There was one guy in it, in the driver's seat, and he had his head down on the steering wheel.

Moving swiftly, I crossed over to

the trash can and reached in and got the gun and walked back down the side street to my car.

At home, I drove the car into the basement garage and shoved the gun up on one of the hot air ducts that ran overhead from the furnace. Later I'd dispose of it permanently.

Upstairs in the dark kitchen, I found a bottle of rye in a cabinet and took a long pull from the bottle. The whisky burned in my throat and flared like phosphorus in my stomach. I waited in the darkness, gagging, until the heat had subsided to a diffusive warmth, and then I went through the living room to the front hall and upstairs to the bedroom.

Meg was asleep on her side in her twin bed. If she was not asleep, she pretended that she was. Moonlight slanted through the half-shut slats of the blinds and flowed along the contour of her rounded hip. I found pajamas in a drawer of my chest and undressed beside my bed. Lying on my back, I looked up at the ceiling and thought about everything that had happened. There was nothing, even then, that I wanted changed. And that was good, at least, because it was far too late for change, even if I'd wanted it.

I didn't sleep. I was still lying on my back, in the position I had first taken, when the electric alarm went off beside Meg's bed. It was the first time I'd ever known her to set the alarm.

I lay silently with my eyes half open and watched her silence the alarm and swing out of bed. She went over to the bathroom door and snapped on the light inside, and I could see against it, through the sheer stuff of her nightgown, the lithe loveliness of her body. She closed the door behind her, and the shower began running in its stall. After about five minutes, she came back into the bedroom and turned on the small lights on both sides of her dressing table mirror. Sitting on the bench before the mirror, turned a little to the side so that I was looking at her profile, she began to paint her nails. The sheer robe that had replaced her gown fell open across her thighs from its narrow belt, and she crossed her knees, resting each hand palm down on the upper knee as she painted the nails with the little brush that was fastened to the stopper of the bottle. She worked very slowly and carefully. She didn't look in my direction at all.

When the paint on her nails was dry, she turned on the bench and began to brush her hair with long, even strokes. She brushed the hair until it shone like white gold in the light. When she lifted the brush to the crown of her head to start the long sweep down the fall of her hair, I could see clearly in the glass the firm protrusion of her breasts against the thin robe.

The stroking done, she lay the brush down on the glass top of the table and picked up a thin gold tube of lip rouge. She applied the scarlet stuff to her lips in a bright smear, leaning forward to look into the mirror, smoothing it with the tip of a little finger and tucking her lips in together to give it the shape of her mouth. Standing, she loosened the robe and let it drift down in a thin cloud over the bench behind her.

Naked, she padded across the room to the closet, gathering clothing. Carrying the garments, she came back to her bed and began to dress. In a couple of frail black wisps, she sat on the side of the bed and smoothed nylon onto her long legs, holding each leg in turn out stiffly with the toes pointed, bending far forward from the hips to draw her hands up slowly from the ankle along calf and thigh. Standing again, she lowered a soft black dress over her head. The dress was slashed low in front, a narrow V between her breasts, and was like lacquer on her hips. In high-heeled sandals, she returned to the mirror and repaired her hair, looking at herself with quiet appraisal in the glass. Then she turned and went out of the room.

She still hadn't looked at me. Not even briefly.

I kept on lying there in bed, and pretty soon the good smell of coffee came up the stairs and into the room, and for just a second it was a morning like any other morning, with the paper to read and a trip to the office around nine. I lifted my arms back and above my head, stretching, feeling the muscles pull tight along the length of my body. I showered and dressed and went down.

Meg was in the breakfast room. She was standing at the wide window overlooking the back lawn, and I saw that she was holding a cup of coffee in her hands. I went up behind her and put my hands on her shoulders, but she was still as stiff as wood, and the chill of her flesh came through her dress into my fingers.

"There's coffee on the sideboard," she said.

"Thanks."

I went over and poured coffee into a cup. I carried the cup over to the table and sat down. Meg still stood at the window with her back to me, looking out into the bright sunshine of the morning. The steam from my coffee ascended into my nostrils. It was a good smell. It was a smell a man might miss if he were never to know it again.

"You said bourbon," Meg said. "You said his bourbon wasn't dry on the carpet."

I looked down into the black liquid with the steam rising lazily from its surface. "Bourbon's a word, honey. You see a man taking a drink, you say, 'Look at that man drinking bourbon.' It stands for anything."

She shook her head. "No. You say highball, or cocktail, or just drink. You don't say bourbon, or rye, or scotch, unless you know for sure it's bourbon, or rye, or scotch. That's why you said bourbon, Hank, because you knew it was bourbon. Because you saw him mix it and even had one with him out of the glass that was sitting on the little table at the end of the sofa. That was the first time you were there, Hank. The time you killed him."

She stood waiting for me to say something, but I had nothing to say, because there was no use in confessing something she already knew, and there was no use lying when a lie would do no good.

After a while, she said quietly, "I've been wondering why you came back. I think it must have been because you saw me arrive and didn't want me to get into trouble. I think it was because you love me very much. I think that's why you stayed and called the police, too. Because you love me, I mean. Because you thought I wouldn't think you'd killed him if you did a thing like that. It was an awful chance to take."

She turned then and faced me, the bright glass behind her, looking at me with eyes that were dead, holding the fragile cup in her hands below her breasts.

"I've committed adultery," she said softly. "You killed Bruce Caldwell because you thought the killing was a way to get me back. I ought to be grateful for such a love." She stopped, looking at me across the cradled cup, and when she spoke again her voice was no more than a whisper. "But I'm not. I'm very sorry, but I loved Bruce so much that there's nothing I want now but to see his murderer dead."

The tiredness inside me was like nothing I'd ever known before. "That's a lot of love," I said.

"I'm very confused," she answered. She shook her head and came beside my chair. "You were wrong in what you did, but you didn't know you were — and you did it for me. I wonder . . . I wonder if you would like to have me one more time."

I looked up at her, at the strange blankness on her face, the beautiful body that was freshly bathed and clothed. I understood the ritual she had performed now, as nearly as such things can be understood. She came to me, and she was stiff and cold, the way a woman can be when she is giving herself in payment for something.

And when it was all over, I was not surprised to find a gun in her hand pointing at my head.

Day's Work

An accident's a terrible thing. The two men couldn't get over it for a long time . . .

BY JONATHAN LORD

THEY were walking toward the waterfront area, walking quietly, when they heard the car hit the kid. They stopped short at the sound of the kid's scream, and then they began to run toward the accident.

They were quietly dressed, conservative-looking men, lean and hard-muscled and in perfect condition, and they didn't puff or get out of breath. As they ran, the taller man said, "It sounded like a bad one." He had blond hair, blue eyes, and thin, sensitive features, and there was a look of shock on his face as he stared ahead through the darkness.

The other man was very short, just a shade over five feet, and his hair and eyes were dark. "Yeah," he said. "That car was going plenty fast." He added softly, "Hell of a thing, street accidents."

They turned a corner, and the accident was right there before them. The kid was about ten or eleven, lying stiff and unmoving, his body thrown a full foot ahead of the front wheels of the car. The driver stood alongside the car, his face chalk-white and his lips twitching, staring at the kid and at the gathering crowd, and then back at the kid. "I didn't even see him," he said. "He come running out from between two parked cars . . ."

The blond man stepped forward, looking at the crowd. "Anybody send for an ambulance?" he asked.

A woman in the crowd answered him. "Man went to call one," she said. "Ain't no use, though — the kid's gone. I saw the whole thing. I . . ."

"You never can tell," the blond man said. "Doctors can do wonderful things, sometimes. You never can tell." He stared down at the kid. "I wonder if we ought to move him, cover him or something."

"Better not," the short man said. "If he *is* still alive, you can harm him by moving him." He looked down at the kid, and then turned his face away. "Hell of a thing, huh, Joe? A little kid like that . . ."

The blond man's eyes caught the driver's, and the driver took a blind step forward, toward him. "I didn't even see him," the driver said. "He come out suddenly . . ." He stopped short as the blond man turned away.

Then a police car arrived, with the ambulance right behind it, and the two men stepped away, into the crowd. They stood watching, sadly, as an interne examined the boy briefly and placed a sheet over his body.

"We better go," the short man said. "We don't want to be late."

The blond man glanced at his watch, a thin-gold, expensive timepiece. "We won't be late," he said. "We've got an hour. Mr. Conners said he won't be there until eleven."

They stood watching a few minutes longer. Then they walked away, headed again for the waterfront area, walking silently for almost two blocks. Finally the short man said, "Things like that break your heart."

The blond man nodded. "Kid was just about the same age as my oldest," he said.

"Mine, too," the short man said. "Scares the hell out of a father, seeing something like that."

The blond man nodded again. "Worst thing is," he said, "there isn't a damn thing you can do about it. You can't expect a ten-year-old kid to hang around the house all day, and you can't expect the kid to hang around his mother all day, either. You've just got to pound it into his head about being careful when he crosses the streets — and then you keep your fingers crossed."

"That's the rub, all right," the short man said. "I ever catch one of my kids crossing in the middle of the street, I'll pound his can so he won't sit down for a month."

They were deep in the waterfront area now, and the streets were shabby and rundown and completely deserted. They continued walking, talking softly, until they reached the water's edge.

"This is the spot, right here," the blond man said. "The boat's supposed to come in over there, near that painted line."

"We better get in the shadows," the short man said.

There was darkness just a few feet

to the left of them, off where the street light did not penetrate, and they walked over until the shadows enclosed them, waiting for the third man to show up. He came after they'd waited fifteen minutes.

He was extremely tall, much taller than the other two, and dressed in the same quiet, conservative way, but his clothes were a bit shabbier than theirs, and he was very nervous. He stopped at the water's edge, looked at his watch, and then stood staring out at the water.

The men in shadows stood watching him for a moment, and then the blond man stepped forward. "Better forget the boat, Marty," he said.

The man at the water's edge turned and stared at him, sick fear on his face.

"Better forget the boat," the blond man said. "You won't be on it tonight."

The tall man's lips were trembling now, and he pressed them together to steady them. He said, finally, "Give me a break, Joe . . ."

"No breaks," the blond man said.

"For God's sakes, Joe," the tall man said, "act like a human being — let me get on that boat. Who the hell will ever know? I'll spend the rest of my life out of the country. Jesus, Joe, we grew up together — we been friends twenty years."

The blond man shook his head. "You shouldn't have done it," he said. "We stopped being friends when Mr. Conners gave us the order on you this afternoon. No breaks, Marty."

The tall man stared at him for a moment, and then, hopelessly, he shrugged his shoulders.

"Maybe you better turn around, Marty," the blond man said, softly.

The tall man turned his back, and then, abruptly, began to run. He had taken four steps when a bullet cut him down, onto his knees. There were three more shots and he cried out once, softly, and fell forward on his face.

The two men walked up to the body, and the blond man turned the dead one over with the toe of his shoe and studied him for a moment. "All right," he said. "Let's get the guns into the drink, and move." The guns made gentle splashes as they hit.

The men waited a moment longer, to make sure there were no footsteps approaching, and then they left. They did not run; they walked away slowly and in silence.

They were silent again for almost two blocks, and then the short man said, "I just can't get that accident out of my mind. Awful thing to see."

"Awful," the blond man said. "I hope they give that driver twenty years. Imagine the bastard — driving fast on a dark night like this." He shook his head. "I better have another talk with my kids first thing tomorrow morning."

Joey was murdered, and so was the Chinese exporter. Cordell went to work to see if there was a connection between them.

A Matt Cordell Story

BY EVAN HUNTER

Good and Dead

He was a small man, small in stature and small in social significance. Another bum, another wino, another panhandler. A nobody.

But he was Joey, and we'd shared the warmth of many a doorway together, tilted the remains of countless bottles of smoke together, worked the Bowery from end to end like partners, like friends.

He was Joey, but he was dead.

He was tattered in death, as he had been when alive. His clothes were baggy and ill-fitting, rumpled with the creases of park benches and cold pavements, stinking with the sweat of Summer's heat, crawling with the legged jewels of the poor.

I stared down at him, and I thought small thoughts because thinking must always be a small thing in the presence of death.

"Shall we get the cops, Matt?" someone asked.

I nodded and kept looking at Joey and at the bright stain of blood on the side of his head, the matted hair soggy and dirt-encrusted, where the bullet had entered.

Cooper Square, and the statue of Peter Cooper looked down with bronze aloofness, hemmed in by a grilled fence, surrounded by empty park benches. Cooper Square, and a Summer night as black as a raven's wing, sprinkled with the dazzle of stars that Joey would never see again.

I felt empty.

"Why'd anyone want to kill a bum, Matt?" one of the boys asked.

"I don't know," I said. Across the street, the squat structure that was Cooper Union fought with the Third Avenue El for dominance of the sky. A boy and a girl hugged the shadows of the building, walking their way slowly toward the small park and the cluster of winos. There was a mild breeze on the air, a Summer breeze that touched the skin with delicate feminine hands. There was a hum on the air, too, the hum of voices on fire escapes, of people crowding the streets, of the day dying as Joey had died.

And over the hum came the wail of a siren, and the winos faded back into the anonymity of the Bowery, blending with the shadows, merging with the pavements and the ancient buildings, turning their backs on the law.

I turned my back, too.

I walked away slowly as the siren got louder. I didn't turn for another look. I didn't *want* another look.

II

Chink was waiting for me outside the flophouse I'd called home for close to three months.

He was standing in the shadows, and I'd have missed him if he hadn't whispered, "Matt?"

I stopped and peered into the darkened doorway. "Who's that?"

"Me. Chink."

"What is it?"

"You got a minute, Matt?"

"I've got a lifetime. What is it?"

"Joey."

"What about him?"

"You were friends, no?"

I stared into the darkness, trying to see Chink's face. It was rumored that he came originally from Shanghai and that he could speak twelve Chinese dialects. It was also rumored that he'd been a big man in China before he came to the States, that he'd come here because of a woman who'd two-timed him in the old country. That gave us a common bond.

"You *were* friends, weren't you, Matt?"

"We were friends. So?"

"You know what happened?"

"I know he was killed."

"Do you know why?"

"No." I paused and stepped into the doorway, and there was the sickish smell of opium about Chink, overpowering in the small hallway. "Do you?"

"No."

"Then why the hell are you wasting my time?"

"I got an idea, Matt."

"I'm listening."

"Are you interested?"

"What the hell are you driving at, Chink? Spit it out."

"Joey. I think he was killed for some reason."

"That's brilliant, Chink. That's real . . ."

"I mean, I don't think this was just an ordinary mugg and slug, you follow? This was a setup kill."

"How do you figure?"

"I think Joey saw too much."

"Go smoke your pipe, Chink," I said. I started to shove past him. "Joey was usually too drunk to see his own hand in front of . . ."

"Harry Tse," Chink said.

It sounded like Harry Shoe. "Who's Harry Shoe?"

"He was killed the other night, Matt. You heard about it, didn't you?"

"No."

"They thought it was a tong job. Harry was big in his own tong."

"What is this: Fu Manchu?"

"Don't joke, Matt."

"Okay, Chink, no jokes. What makes you think they tie?"

"Something Joey said when I told him about Harry."

"When was this?"

"Yesterday. He said, '*So that's who it was.*' "

"That doesn't mean a damned thing, Chink."

"Or it could mean a lot."

"Stop being inscrutable. So it means a lot, or it means nothing. Who gives a rat's backside?"

"I thought Joey was your friend."

"He was. He's dead now. What do you want me to do? The cops are already on it."

"You used to be a shamus."

"Used to be, is right. No more. Joey's dead. The cops'll get his killer."

"You think so? They're already spreading talk he fell and cracked his head that way even though there's a bullet hole in him. They say he was drunk. You think they're gonna give a damn about one bum more or less."

"But you do, huh, Chink? You give a damn."

"I do."

"Why? What difference does it make to you?"

"Joey was good to me." His voice trailed off. "He was good to me, Matt." There was a catch in his voice, as if he were awed by the idea of *anybody* being good to him.

"The good die young," I said. "Let me by, Chink. I need some sleep."

"You're . . . you're not going to do anything about it?"

"I guess not. Maybe. I don't know. I'll think about it. Good-night, Chink."

I started up the stairs and Chink yelled, "He was your friend, too, Matt. Just remember that. Just remember it."

"Sure," I said.

It took me a long time to forget it. I still hadn't forgotten by the time I fell asleep.

The morning was hot and sticky. My shirt stuck to my back and my skin was feverish and gummy, and I wanted to crawl out of it like a snake. I dug up a bottle of wine, taking four drinks before one would stay down. I faced the morning then, blinking at the fiery sun, wishing for a beach, or a mountain lake, or even a breeze. There was none. There was only the El, rusted and gaunt, and the baking pavements. I started walking, heading for Chinatown because things can look different in the blaze of a new day.

I found Chink. He was lying on a pad, and there was opium in his eyes and the slack tilt of his mouth.

He looked up at me sleepily, and then grinned blandly.

"Hello, Matt."

"This Harry Shoe," I said.

"Harry Tse."

"Yeah. Any survivors?"

"His wife. Lotus Tse. Why, Matt? You going to do something? You going to get Joey's killer?"

"Where is she? Tse's wife."

"On Mott Street. Here, Matt, I'll give you the address." He reached behind him for a brush, dipped it into a pot of ink and scrawled an address on a brown piece of paper. "Tell her I sent you, Matt. Tell her Charlie Loo sent you."

"Is that your name?"

He nodded.

"All right, Charlie. I'll see you."

"Good luck, Matt."

"Thanks."

I knocked on the door and waited, and then I knocked again.

"Who is it?" The voice had a sing-song lilt, like a mild breeze rustling through a willow tree. It brought pictures of an ancient China, a land of delicate birds and eggshell skies, colorful kimonos and speckled white stallions.

"I'm a friend of Charlie Loo," I said to the closed door.

"Moment."

I waited a few more minutes, and when the door opened, I was glad I had. She was small, with shiny black hair that tumbled to her shoulders, framing an oval face. Her eyes tilted sadly, brown as strong coffee, fringed with soot-black lashes. She had a wide mouth, and she wore a silk blouse and a skirt that hugged her small, curving hips.

"Yes, please?"

"May I come in?"

"All right." The sing-song made it sound like a question. She stepped aside, and I walked into the apartment, through a pair of beaded drapes, into a living room that was cool with the shade of the building that crowded close to the open window.

"My name is Matt Cordell," I said.

"You are a friend of Charlie's?"

"Yes."

"I see. Sit down, Mr. Cordell."

"Thank you." I slouched into an easy chair, clenched my hands over my knees. "Your husband, Mrs. Tse. What do you know about his death?"

Her eyes widened a little, but her face remained expressionless otherwise. "Is that why you are here?"

"Yes."

She shrugged small shoulders. "He . . . was killed. Is there more to say?"

"How?"

"A knife."

"When?"

"Tuesday night."

"Today is Friday," I said, thinking aloud.

"Is it?" she asked. There was such a desperate note in her voice that I looked up suddenly. She was not watching me. She was staring through the open window at the brick wall of the opposite building.

"Do you have any idea who did it?"

"The tong, they say. I don't know."

"You don't think it was a tong?"

"No. No, I don't think so. I . . . I don't know what to think."

"What did your husband do?"

"Export-import. His business was good. He was a good man, my husband. A good man."

"Any enemies?"

"No. No, I don't know any."

"Did he seem worried about anything?"

"No. He was happy."

I took a deep breath. "Well, is there anything you can tell me? Anything that might help in . . ."

She shook her head, dangerously close to tears. "You . . . you do not understand, Mr. Cordell. Harry was a happy man. There was nothing. No reason. No . . . reason to kill him. No reason."

I waited a moment before asking the next question. "Was he ever away from home? I mean, any outside friends? A club? Bowling team? Band? Anything like that?"

"Yes."

"What?"

"A club. He went on Mondays. He was well-liked."

"What's the name of the club?"

"Chinese Neighborhood Club. Incorporated, I think. Yes. It's on Mulberry Street. I don't know the address."

"I'll find it," I said, rising. "Thank you, Mrs. Tse. I appreciate your help."

"Are you looking for Harry's murderer, Mr. Cordell?"

"I think so."

"Find him," she said simply.

Her eyes were dry as she made a movement of dismissal.

III

The Chinese Neighborhood Club, Inc. announced itself to the sidewalk by means of a red and black lettered sign swinging on the moist Summer breeze. A narrow entranceway huddled beneath the sign, and two Chinese stood alongside the open doorway, talking softly, their Panamas tilted back on their heads. They glanced at me as I started up the long narrow stairway.

The stairwell was dark. I followed the creaking steps, stopping at a landing halfway up. There were more steps leading to another landing, but I decided I'd try the door on this landing first. I didn't bother to knock. I took the knob, twisted it, and the door opened.

The room was almost unfurnished. There was a long curtained closet on one wall, and an easy chair just inside the doorway. A long table ran down the center of the room. A man was seated at the table. A stringed instrument rested on the table before him, looking very much like a small harp. The man had the withered parchment face of a Chinese mandarin. He held two sticks with felted tips in his hands. A small boy with jet black hair stood alongside the table. They both looked up as I came into the room.

"Yes?" the old man asked.

"I'm looking for friends of Harry Tse."

"O.K." the old man said. He whispered something to the boy, and the kid tossed me a darting glance, and then went out the door through which I'd entered. The door closed behind him and I sat in the easy chair while the old man began hitting the strings of his instrument with the two felted sticks. The music was Old China. It twanged on the air in discordant cacophony, strangely fascinating, harsh on the ears, but somehow soothing. It droned on monotonously, small staccato bursts that vibrated the strings, set the air humming.

The sticks stopped, and the old man looked up.

"You *who?*" he asked.

"Matt Cordell."

"Yes. Mmm, yes."

He went back to his instrument. The room was silent except for the twanging of the strings. I closed my eyes and listened, remembering a time when Trina and I had found the wonder of Chinatown, found it for our very own. That had been a happy time, with our marriage as bright as the day outside. That had been before I'd found her in Garth's arms, before I'd smashed in his face with the butt of my .45. The police had gone easy on me. Trina and Garth had dropped charges, but it was still assault with a deadly weapon, and the police had yanked my license from me, and Matt Cordell had drifted to the Bowery along with the other derelicts. Trina and Garth? Mexico, the stories said, for a quick divorce. Leaving behind them a guy who didn't give a damn anymore.

I listened to the music, and I thought of the liquor I'd consumed since then, the bottles of sour wine, the smoke, the canned heat. I thought of the flophouses, and the hallways, and the park benches and the gutters and the stink and filth of the Bowery. A pretty picture, Matt Cordell. A real pretty picture.

Like Joey.

Only Joey was dead, really dead. I was only close to it.

The music stopped. There was the bare room again, and the old man, and the broken memories.

"Is someone coming to talk to me?" I asked.

"You go up," the old man said. "Upstairs. You go. Someone talk to you."

"Thanks," I said.

I went into the hallway, wondering why the old man had sent the kid up ahead of me. Probably a natural distrust of Westerners. Whoever was up there had been warned that an outsider was in the house. I climbed the steps, and found another doorway at the landing.

I opened the door.

The room was filled with smoke. There were at least a dozen round tables in the room, and each table was crowded with seated Chinese. There was a small wooden railing that separated the large room from a small office with a desk. A picture of Chiang Kai-shek hung on one wall. A fat man sat at the desk with his back to me. The kid who'd been downstairs was standing alongside him. I turned my back to the railing and the desk and looked into the room. A few of the men looked up, but most went on with what I supposed were their games.

The place was a bedlam of noise. Each man sitting at the tables held a stack of tiles before him. As far as I could gather, the play went in a clockwise motion, with each player lifting a tile and banging it down on the table as he shouted something in Chinese. I tried to get the gist of the game, but it was too complicated. Every now and then, one man would raise a pointed stick and push markers across wires stretched over the tables — like the markers in a pool room. A window stretched across the far end of the room, and one group of men at a table near the window were the quietest in the room. They were playing cards, and from a distance, it looked like good, old-fashioned poker.

I turned away from them and stared at the back of the man seated at the desk. I cleared my throat.

He swung his chair around, grinning broadly, exposing a yellow gold tooth in the front of his mouth.

"Hello, hello," he said.

I gestured over my shoulder with my head. "What's that? Mahjong?"

He peered around as if he hadn't seen the wholesale gaming. "Chinese game," he said.

"Thanks," I said. "Did Harry Tse play it?"

"Harry? No, Harry play poker. Far table. You know Harry?"

"Not exactly."

The Chinese shook his head, and the fat of his chin waddled. "Harry dead."

"I know."

"Yes. Dead." He shook his head again.

"Was he here last Monday night?"

"Oh sure. He here every Monday."

"Did he play poker?"

"Oh sure. He always play. Harry good guy."

"Who played with him?"

"Hmm?"

"Last Monday? Who was he playing with?"

"Why?"

"He was killed. Maybe one of his friends did it. Who did he play with?"

The fat Chinese stood up abruptly and looked at the far table. He nodded his head then. "Same ones. Always play poker. Only ones." He pointed at the far table. "They play with Harry."

"Thanks. Mind if I ask them a few questions?"

The fat Chinese shrugged, so I started into the room past the Mahjong tables and heading for the men playing poker. Four men were seated at the table. None of them looked up when I stopped alongside.

I cleared my throat.

A thin man with short black hair and a clean-shaven face looked up curiously. His eyes were slanted, his skin pulled tight at the corners. He held his cards before him in a wide fan.

"My name's Cordell," I said to him. "I understand Harry Tse was playing cards here the night before he was killed."

"Yes?" the thin man asked.

"Are you the spokesman for the group?"

"I'll do. What's on your mind?"

"Who won Monday night?"

The thin man thought this over. He shrugged and turned to another player. "Who won, Tommy?"

Tommy was a husky boy with wide jowls. He shrugged, too. "I don't remember, Lun."

"That your name?" I asked the first guy.

"That's right. Lun Ching."

"Who won, Lun Ching?"

"I don't remember."

"Did Harry win?"

"I don't think so."

"Yes or no?"

"No."

"Are you sure?"

Lun Ching stared at me. "Are you from the police?"

"No."

He nodded his head imperceptibly. "Harry didn't win. That's enough for you." He turned back to his cards, fished two from the fan and said to a player across the table, "Two cards."

The dealer threw two cards onto the table, and Lun Ching reached for them. I reached at the same time, clamping my fingers onto his wrist.

"I'm not through yet, Lun."

He shook his hand free, and shoved his chair back. "You better get the hell out of here, Mac," he said.

"Matt," I corrected. "I want to know who won here Monday night. You going to tell me?"

"What difference does it make?"

"I want to know."

Lun gestured impatiently with his head. "Tommy won."

I turned to the husky jowled Chinese. "Did you?"

"Yes."

"How much?"

"A few bucks."

"Did Harry lose?"

"Yes."

"How much?"

"I don't know. Two, three dollars."

"Who else won?"

"What?"

"You said you'd won a few bucks, Tommy. You also said Harry lost about three bucks. What did the rest of you do?"

Lun Ching stood up. "We broke even. Does that answer you?"

"Maybe," I said. I turned and started across the room. Over my shoulder, I said, "I might come back."

Someone from the table whispered, "Don't hurry."

I stopped at the desk behind the wooden railing, and the fat Chinese looked up.

"I don't think I caught your name," I said.

"Wong. Sam Wong."

"Mr. Wong, did Harry leave here alone on Monday night?"

"Yes, he did."

"Did he say where he was going? Did he have to meet anyone?"

"No. He didn't say. I think he go home."

"I see."

Sam Wong looked at me curiously. "Harry no killed Monday night," he said, his voice puzzled. "Harry killed Tuesday night."

"I know," I said. "That's what's bothering me."

IV

None of it fit.

I was banging my head against a stone wall, and I didn't like the feeling. It wasn't like the old days when someone shoved a fat retainer under my nose, held it out like a carrot to a rabbit, challenged me to find a missing husband or squelch a bit of blackmail.

There was no retainer. Only the thought of Joey lying dead in the small park, Joey about whom I knew practically nothing. He'd been driven by some ghost, too, and the ghost was a thirsty one. We shared the Big Thirst, and we'd done our damnedest to quench it, doing whatever we could to get the necessary money. I thought of the last bottle I'd shared with Joey. We'd sat on the corner of my cot a few days back, drinking the fifth of Imperial, forgetting the heated streets outside, forgetting everything but the driving desire to get blind, stinking drunk.

Now Joey was dead, and Charlie had suggested a tie-in between that and the death of Harry Tse, a man I didn't know at all. A sensible guy would have called it a day. A sensible guy would have said, "*All right, you stupid bastard, your first idea was wrong. Harry Tse didn't win any money, and that's not why he was killed. There was another reason, and it wasn't a cheating wife because her love is stamped all over her face. So give it up and rustle a bottle of smoke, give it up and forget it.*"

I'd stopped being sensible a long time ago. I'd stopped the night I took Garth's face apart.

I shook my head and bummed a dime from the next guy who passed. That bought me a glass of beer, and that cleared my head a little, and I was ready to play shamus again even though it was too hot to be playing anything.

I started walking through Chinatown, looking for an idea. I passed the windows crammed with herbs and roots, crammed with fish and spice and fowl. I passed the other windows brimming with sandals and kimonos and jade and beads and boxes and figurines and fans. I passed the newstands displaying Chinese periodicals and newspapers. I passed the restaurants, upstairs, downstairs, level with the street. I passed them all in a miasma of heat that clung to the narrow streets like a living thing.

And no idea came.

The heat stifled thought. It crawled around the open throat of my shirt, stained my armpits, spread sweat across my back muscles. It was too hot to walk, and too hot to think, and too damned hot to do anything but sidle up to a beer glass beaded with cold drops.

But I had to think, so I forced the heat out of my mind and I tried to remember what Mrs. Tse had told me about her husband, Harry.

Export-import.

I stopped in the nearest candy store, waded through two dozen Tses in the phone book and finally located his business address, right in the center of Chinatown where I'd hoped it would be. I sighed against the heat, wiped the sweat from my forehead and headed for his office.

It was upstairs. A small unimportant office with an important-looking title on the door: *Harry Tse: Exports — Imports.* I tried the knob, half-expecting the office to be closed. The door opened, and I found myself in a small reception room. A desk hugged the wall, and a Chinese girl hugged the desk. She looked up when I came in, her sloe eyes frankly appraising me.

She was dressed like any girl you'd see in the subway, maybe even more so. She was small, the way most Chinese women are, but there was nothing slight or delicate about her. The dress clinging to her was green silk, and it slashed low between her breasts, ending in a rhinestone clip somewhere above her navel. She wore no makeup. A splash of lipstick had been wiped across her full mouth, and her lips parted now as I walked to the desk.

"My name is Matt Cordell," I said.

A spark of interest flickered in her eyes, died, and then rekindled itself to smolder like a burning coal. "Yes?" She wet her lips with the tip of her tongue. "May I help you, sir?"

"Mrs. Tse sent me," I lied. "What do you know about her husband?"

"You're investigating his murder?"

"More or less," I said. She looked at me dubiously and then she shrugged. The open V of her blouse moved a fraction of an inch. I stared at her, but her eyes met mine frankly and levelly.

"I don't know anything about his murder."

"What about his habits?"

"What about them?"

"Do you know where he was going on the night he was killed?"

"Yes. One of his clients lives on West 72nd Street. I think he was going there. In fact, I'm sure he was."

"What's your job here?"

"Receptionist, secretary, all-around girl."

"What does that include?"

"Just what it sounded like." She arched one eyebrow onto her forehead. "Harry was married. I know his wife, and I respect her."

"I see."

"Harry was walking up to 14th for some air. Before he left the office, he told me that. He never reached the Subway on Fourteenth. He was killed outside Cooper Union."

"Where Joey was killed," I said.

"Who? Oh yes, Joey. Charlie Loo's friend."

"You knew Joey?"

"No." She swung her legs out from the desk, and her skirt rode up over her knees. She glanced down at the skirt, but didn't move to touch it. "No, I didn't know Joey. Charlie told me about what he'd said, though. He figured there might be a connection."

"Do *you* think so?"

She shrugged again, and this time the V moved more than a fraction of an inch. She kept talking, her hands caressing the rhinestone clip at the apex of the V. "I don't know. I passed it on to Mrs. Tse. She said she was going to look up Charlie and get him to point out this Joey person to her. She said she wanted to ask him what he'd seen."

"When was this?"

"Yesterday, I think. I don't really remember. There's been so damned much confusion around here . . ." She stopped abruptly and suddenly crossed her legs. She leaned over and took off one of her high heels, and the V of her dress just didn't give one good goddamn anymore. "New shoes," she said. "Tight."

I stood up and walked over to the desk. She lifted her head to look up at me, and she wet her lips again.

"Honey," I said, "you're looking for trouble."

When her voice came, it was low and steady. "Maybe I want trouble. It gets boring sitting around here all alone all day."

I considered this and then turned for the door. She rose like a cat, crossing the room before me, and trying to flatten herself against the door. She tried, but she didn't succeed, because a body like that would have trouble flattening itself against anything.

"Come on," I said, "cut the dramatics. I'm leaving."

With a quick movement, she turned and snapped the lock on the door. When she turned back to me, the rhinestone clip was gone. She tossed it up and down on the palm of her hand, and the movement of her shoulders and her body rippled the front of the dress.

There was the age-old look on her face, the look that had been spawned before Man knew how to build a fire. She took a step closer, and I suddenly forgot all about the heat and Joey and Harry and everybody and everything in the world. There was only the tilt of her eyes and the moistness of her mouth, and then she was in my arms and I buried my lips in her throat and listened to the hum of traffic and people outside.

I left her much later and went down to the street again. I started walking, and I'd walked for two blocks before I realized I was being followed. I quickened my pace, and the sweat sprang out all over my body. I followed the narrow, twisting streets, ducking into an alley and sprinting for the other end. I hadn't counted on my followers knowing Chinatown better than I did.

I almost smashed into them at the other end of the alley.

I had a chance to recognize Lun Ching and his pal Tommy, and then a fist lashed out, surprisingly forceful for the thin man who threw it. I doubled over, feeling the heat and the drinking I'd done for a long time now.

"You son of a bitch," Lun shouted.

I lifted my face in time to see the sap in his hand. Then the sap went up over his head and came down on the side of my neck, knocking me flat against one wall of the alley. I grabbed at the bricks for support, but the sap was up and down again, and this time it peeled back a half inch of flesh from my cheek.

"You're going to the morgue, you bastard," Lun said. He brought back the sap, and this time I fell to my knees and Tommy kicked me quickly and expertly. Lun bent over me and the sap became a sledge hammer now, up and down, hitting me everywhere, on my shoulders, my face, my upraised hands and arms.

"Break up the card game, will you? Come acting tough, huh?"

And always the sap, up and down, viciously pounding me closer and closer to the cement until my head was touching it and Tommy's kick to my temple made everything black.

V

The brick wall was a mile high. It stretched out above me and leaned dangerously against the sky. I watched it, wondering when it would fall, and after a while I realized it wasn't going to fall at all.

I stumbled to my knees then and touched the raw pain that was my face. I ached everywhere, and I ached more when I remembered Lun and Charlie. But I wasn't angry at them. They'd given me a hell of a beating, but they'd also given me an idea, and it was an idea any stupid bastard should have got all by himself. So I filed them away under unfinished business and stumbled my way out of the alley. Lun Ching had said I was going to the morgue, and he was right.

It was cool.

I thanked the respite from the heat and followed the attendant down the long, gloomy corridor.

"This is it," he said.

He pulled out the drawer and I looked down into Joey's lifeless face, at the flabby whiskey sodden features that even death could not remove.

"That's him," I said.

"Sure, I know it's him," the attendant answered, his voice echoing off the walls.

"I . . . I wondered about his personal effects."

"You a relative?"

"No. I don't think he had any relatives. I was his friend."

"Mmmm." The attendant considered this deeply. "Not a hell of a lot there, you know. Sent them all up to Homicide because they're still investigating this. Got a list, though, and I can tell you what was on him."

"I'd appreciate that."

"Sure. No trouble at all." I followed him to a desk at the end of the corridor. He sat down and picked up a clipboard, and then began flipping the pages. "Let's see. Yeah, here he is, Joseph H. Gunder."

I hadn't even known Joey's last name. The anonymity of the Bowery is almost complete.

"Yeah, he didn't have much," the attendant said. "Want me to read them off?"

"Yes, please."

"A dollar bill, and thirty-five cents in change. Want that broken down?"

"No, that's fine."

"Okay, let's see. Handkerchief, switch knife, pint of Carstair's almost empty, some rubber bands, package of Camels — two butts in it. Wallet with identification. That's it."

"A pint of Carstairs?" I was thinking of the fifth of Imperial Joey had brought to me and how we'd killed it.

"Yep, that's right."

"And . . . and a switch knife?"

"Yeah." He nodded his head.

"And money, too?"

"Say, you want me to repeat the whole damned list?"

"No, that's fine. Thanks." I paused. "Did they decide what killed him?"

"Sure. Hole in the head. Want to see him again?"

"No. I meant, what calibre pistol?"

".22. Why?"

"Just curious. I'll be going."

"Okay, mister. Drop in again some time."

I walked out into the sunshine, away from the moldering bodies. The beginning had been in the morgue then, and I owed Lun Ching a debt. But the end was somewhere else, and I headed there now.

VI

The door opened when I knocked and gave my name.

"I'm sorry," I said. "I just came across something."

"That's all right."

"May I come in?"

"Certainly."

I followed her into the living room again, and I sat down in the same easy chair. I didn't look at the floor or my clenched hands this time. I looked directly at her.

"Ever walk through the Bowery, Mrs. Tse?"

Her eyes were still troubled. She looked at the world through brown curtains that hid the hurt inside her. "Yes."

"Often?"

"I know the neighborhood."

"Do you own a gun, Mrs. Tse?"

She hesitated. "Why . . . yes. Yes, I do."

"A .22, maybe?"

She hesitated again, for a long time. She sighed deeply then and lifted her eyes to mine. There was no expression on her face, and her tone was flat. "You know," she said.

"I know."

She nodded her head aimlessly. "He deserved what he got."

"Joey?"

"Yes. Yes, Joey. He was — your friend, wasn't he?"

"My drinking companion, Mrs. Tse. A man doesn't get to know much about anyone in the Bowery. Nor about what makes them tick."

"How did you know? How did you know I . . . killed him?"

"A few things. A bottle of Imperial, for one. When Joey brought it to me, I never thought to ask where he'd got the money for it. That kind of money doesn't come easy to a bum. When I saw his stuff at the morgue, there was another pint there, and more money. I knew then that Joey had hit it rich recently — and his switch knife told me how."

"Harry was stabbed," she said tonelessly.

"Sure. Joey didn't even know who his victim was. When Charlie mentioned it to him, Joey was probably drunk. He said, '*So that's who it was*' without even thinking. Charlie thought he'd only seen your husband's murderer. He didn't know Joey *was* the murderer."

"And me? How did you come to me?"

"A guess, and a little figuring. A .22 is a woman's gun."

"I have a permit," she said. "I go through the Bowery often. Harry thought . . . he thought I should have one."

"What happened, Mrs. Tse? Do you want to tell me?"

"All right." She paused. "All right. Charlie pointed out your . . . friend to me. I followed him when I left Charlie and I caught up with him in Cooper Square. I asked him what he'd meant by '*So that's who it was.*' He got terribly frightened. He said he hadn't meant to kill Harry. I think he was drunk, I don't know. He said he'd asked Harry for a dime and Harry had refused. He'd pulled a knife and when Harry had started to yell, he stabbed him. For a . . . a dime . . . He stabbed him."

"Go on."

"I couldn't believe it, Mr. Cordell. For a *dime!* I took the gun out of my purse and I just shot him. Only once. Just once. Because he'd stabbed Harry, you see."

"Yes, I understand."

"I shot him," she repeated.

Her voice echoed in the living room, and silence carried it to the walls. She looked up after a while, and her voice was very small now.

"Will you . . . will you take me to the police?"

"No," I said.

"But . . ."

I got to my feet. "Mrs. Tse," I said, "we've never even met."

I walked to the door, leaving her in the living room that faced a blank wall. I took the steps down to the street, leaving her alone because I'd lost someone I loved once and I knew how it felt.

It was hot in the street.

But it was hot where Joey was, too.

Say Goodby to Janie

It was easy to see why Sherman was being framed. He was getting too close to the facts on city corruption — and to the mayor's wife . . .

THAT MORNING on the way to the office I discovered what they were doing to me. As usual I bought the morning paper from the newsdealer on the corner of Division and Fourth. The banner headline jumped up at me.

SHERMAN ACCUSED OF DEMANDING BRIBE.

I stopped dead amid the milling office workers. I read: "Mayor Goodson has suspended Paul Sherman as head of the City Crime Commission, pending a full investigation of the charge by Les Kibby, alleged slot machine king, that Sherman asked Kibby for ten thousand dollars to 'go easy on him.' "

"What is this nonsense?" a bass voice demanded.

Peter B. Warrender was standing beside me. He was one of those gray-haired bankers who made impressive fronts for reform movements. For a year we had worked closely together

A NOVELETTE

BY BRUNO FISCHER

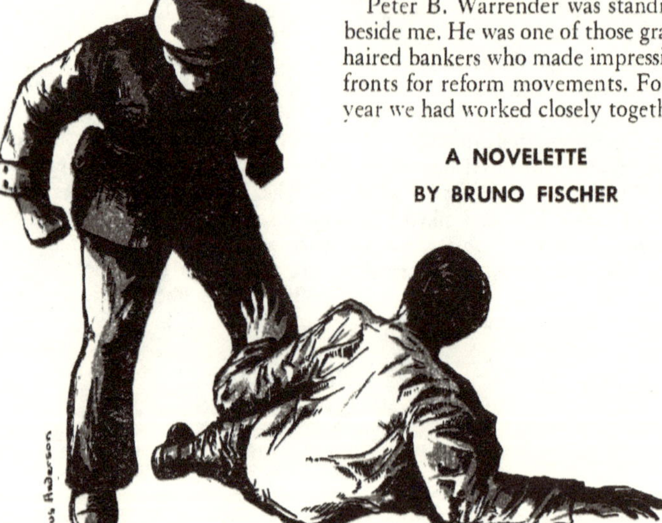

in an organization called Citizens for a Clean City.

"That's exactly what it is — nonsense," I told him. "Kibby has plenty of reason to want to get me."

"But what about the witness?"

I glanced through the rest of the story. The witness was Albert Maurer, one of my own investigators, a man I'd assigned to the gambling racket. He claimed he had overheard me ask Kibby for the money.

"There was bribery, all right," I said. "Maurer sold me out to Goodson."

"The Mayor?" Warrender's aristocratic eyebrows arched. "But why, if he appointed you in the first place?"

"It seems because I'm doing too good a job. Goodson couldn't just fire me. It would raise too much stink. It's better politics to frame me."

On that crowded street, with people pushing by us, Warrender looked me over as if I were a depositor asking for a loan. "Let's hope you can prove it," he said, and marched on to his bank.

It overwhelmed me then, that sense of being trapped and abandoned. If Warrender didn't believe me, who would?

I entered the tall building which housed the modest offices of the Crime Commission. It seemed to me that there was a sudden hush in the lobby as I crossed it to the elevators. A dozen people had stopped whatever they were doing to look at me. I glanced neither right nor left; I stepped into the elevator and took it up to the fourth floor. The operator, who always had a cheery good-morning for me, kept his back to me.

I pushed open the door that said in gilt letters: "CITY CRIME COMMISSION." In the outer office Enid Cooke, who typed the reports and answered the phone, was talking to Albert Maurer.

I strode up to him with blood in my eyes.

Enid said, "Oh!" and Maurer spun around. He saw the look in my face and threw up his arms in front of him and backed against the wall.

"Listen, Mr. Sherman!" he whined.

He was short and dumpy and middle-aged — but a top-notch investigator. I'd considered him the ace of my staff. Now I wanted to tear him apart.

Enid slipped between us. She was a beautiful girl, so tiny that her blonde head hardly reached my shoulders.

"Paul," she said, "they'll jail you for assault."

I drew in my breath to loosen my nerves. "All right, Maurer," I said over her head, "do you stick to your lying story?"

Cowering, he ran his tongue over his lower lip. I knew what his answer would be. He was afraid of me all right, but the most I would do to him would be to clip him a few. Others could do worse.

"I stick to what's so," he said, never taking his nervous, jittery eyes off my face.

I tried to step around Enid to get at him, but she managed to keep in front of me. It was a kind of dance, and during it she said urgently, "Think, Paul. You're letting yourself be sidetracked."

She was right. Mayor Goodson would like me to get myself thrown into jail for beating up this punk. Maurer was a stooge, a pawn. The Mayor himself was the man I was after.

I said bleakly, "Thanks for reminding me," and got out of there.

I left the building. Across the street from the broad plaza stood the million-dollar city hall. Mayor Clyde Goodson had built it for his greater glory and the ten percent kickback from the contractors. I had been closing in on evidence concerning that ten percent, which was the main reason he had made his move against me.

At the foot of the broad city hall steps I saw Janie Jones coming down.

Only, of course, she was no longer Janie Jones, the girl who had lived on the same block with me on the wrong side of the tracks, who had grown up in poverty and used to tell me that she loved me. Now she was Janie Goodson, the wife of the Mayor, and she wore mink.

She stopped several steps above me. She stood tall and graceful in a silver-blue mink stole draped over one shoulder and down her back, and her gray knitted dress flaunted her lovely figure.

"Hello, Janie," I said.

She looked at me with those wide, emotional eyes of hers, and her sensuous lips parted slightly. But she said nothing. Not then. She gathered her stole about her as if suddenly cold, and she came down the rest of the stairs. When she was passing me, she said softly, "Don't do anything foolish," and moved on.

Her image remained vivid in my mind as I went up the steps. I could remember the feel of her waist and hips under my hands, the thrust of her breasts against my chest, the touch of her fingers on my cheek.

This was the bitterest memory of my life.

They were expecting me. Maybe Maurer had tipped them off by phone that I was on my way. They converged on me when I reached the top of the steps. There were three of them — hulking, hard-faced city detectives.

Two grabbed my arms while the third frisked me. They seemed disappointed when they found not even a pen knife on me, but they didn't say so.

Silently and efficiently they bustled me into the building and down a flight of stairs and along a corridor to a small basement room. Only two of them came in with me. The third went off, probably to announce the capture.

"What gives?" I asked.

There was no answer.

2

They remained as silent as they had been all along. One stood planted against the door and the other sat on one of the two wooden chairs at a scarred table. I sat down on the other chair and took out my cigarettes. There was no other furniture in the room, and there was no window.

This was a good place for working a man over, but I didn't think they'd get the order to do so. Mayor Goodson would do nothing crude.

He had made one serious mistake by under-estimating me. I could count on him not doing that again.

He had got to where he was by adhering to the old political adage: if you can't lick 'em, join 'em. He hadn't been able to lick the do-gooders who had organized a year ago into Citizens for a Clean City, and who had made me, a local attorney with a modest practice in civil law, their executive secretary. Nobody questioned that our city was corrupt and gangster-ridden. What was news was that our reform organization was succeeding in rousing the citizens to do something about it come next election.

One evening Mayor Goodson startled us by attending a meeting of our executive board. He said that he heartily approved of our good work and that he was as anxious as anybody to clean up the city. But he needed our help. Our reaction was cold suspicion. He smiled charmingly and said that to show his heart was in the right place he would not only appoint a commission to investigate crime; he would place our executive secretary at the head of it. Meaning me.

We fell for it. Though I suspected a gimmick, I couldn't spot it until after the Crime Commission had been functioning for some time. Then little by little I realized that the Mayor was playing it two ways, neither of which was remotely connected with clean municipal government. He was using the Commission as a facade behind which business went on practically as usual at the old stand, and he was using it to eliminate some of the looters of the city who wanted more than he considered their proper share. We were being tossed scalps that didn't mean very much.

When I got the picture, I set about to change it.

The easiest way for boodle gangs to line their pockets was through construction, such as hospitals or city halls or roads. The most recent big job had been the million-dollar city hall. I put my entire staff on it, and my hunch paid off. The trail led all the way up to the Mayor himself. If he hadn't pocketed all of the hundred thousand dollars in kickbacks from the contractors, he'd retained the lion's share. There was a good reason why he'd become a rich man since entering politics.

All we had to do was prove it. We were examining records and taking depositions when, yesterday morning, I had been called to the Mayor's office.

The Mayor of Coast City had tilted back in his deep leather chair. "Paul," he said, "in this world you've got to have a sense of proportion to get along."

I didn't say anything. This was his office, his speech. I sat on the other side of his desk and watched him roll a cigar between his thick lips. He had a round, chubby face, beginning to run to jowls. Give him another few years in politics and he wouldn't be able to see his shoes for his belly.

I wondered if Janie enjoyed kissing him, enjoyed spending her nights in his bed.

"You're a bright boy," he went on, "but you'll never get far. Anyway, not till you become more realistic."

"Realism," I said, "can be a dirty word."

"That's what I mean — your attitude. I gave you your big chance by appointing you head of the Commission, but you're throwing it away." He sighted me along his cigar. "How'd you like to become district attorney?"

"I'd like it, depending on the price."

"The price," he said, "is to stop tilting against windmills."

I shook my head. "Sorry. That's too high."

Goodson stood up and paced once across the room and back. He was short and dumpy — shorter than Janie. He faced me and said, "What are you after, Paul?"

"To do my job."

"No matter where it leads?"

"Especially no matter where it leads." I crossed my legs. "Of course you can fire me."

His open hand slammed down on the desk. "So that's what you want — to become a martyr and maybe run against me for mayor? Well, by God, I'm not falling into that trap. Now get the hell out of here."

I was opening the door when he said, "Paul." I turned with my hand on the doorknob. He was back in his chair, leaning forward with his elbows on his desk, and within moments his fleshy face seemed to have aged.

"You hate me," he said slowly, "because of Janie. Because I took her away from you."

Maybe he had something there. I didn't know.

"You didn't take her away from me," I told him. "Your money did."

I went out.

Goodson hadn't lost time. As soon as I had left, he must have set about putting pressure on Les Kibby to swear out a statement that I had tried to bribe him, and through either promises or threats he had induced Albert Maurer to say that he had overheard me doing it. And he had been able to suspend me while posing as a knight in shining armor protecting the city from a man who had betrayed the public trust. And now here I was guarded by two silent, frozen-faced detectives in the basement of the million-dollar city hall on which he had cleaned up ten percent for himself and his cronies.

I wasn't in the mood to appreciate the irony.

3

I sat at the scarred table lighting one cigarette from the stub of another and trying to figure out his next move. If I knew him, he had only started on me. He had to break me, crush me, drive me down so low that I would be completely dropped by my own people.

All I could do right now was wait and see.

I waited twenty-eight minutes by my watch. Then the door flew open and Chief of Police George Merkel barged in. He was a raw-boned man with a reputation for being tough.

He hit me in the face before I could rise to my feet. I fell sideways and the chair fell under me. He drew back a foot to kick me in the head. I rolled away from the kick and bounced up quicker than he had expected. I let go with my right. I didn't have Merkel's reputation for being tough, but I had his height and I had youth. I drove him clear across the room, where he collapsed against the wall. Then the two detectives were on me.

For a minute it was quite a scrap. I knew that it wasn't getting me anywhere, that it could turn out only one way, but it did me good to be able to fight back against living, solid flesh and bones. My one regret was that Goodson wasn't in on it.

Merkel recovered enough to come back into the brawl. By that time both chairs and the table had been overturned and I was down on the floor trying to strangle one of the detectives while the other was tugging at my legs. Hands fumbled into my jacket and then I saw a gun flash in front of my face. Merkel held it.

"All right, boys," he said. "Let up."

They climbed to their feet and I did likewise. My collar was askew and my shirt was ripped. I took out my handkerchief and wiped blood from the corner of my mouth. None of the three cops looked in better shape. Merkel in particular sported quite a shiner.

"What was all that for?" I asked.

Merkel showed me the gun in his hand. "Suppose you tell me what this was for?"

It was a Colt .32 automatic with a short, blue-nosed barrel and a checked walnut stock. I had one exactly like it at home.

"What's the pitch?" I demanded.

"I just took it from you," he said almost cheerfully. "You came here to kill the Mayor with it."

Which meant that it was my gun, all right. I had a license for it, so they could prove it was mine by the serial number. While they'd kept me waiting down here, somebody had gone for it, bringing it back.

I said, "You know damn well I didn't have it on me when I came here."

Merkel didn't bother to argue. He opened the door and sang out to somebody in the hall, "Okay, send them down," and returned to the room.

Half a minute later three newspaper reporters and two photographers shoved their way in. I knew them all. I had fed them news releases and statements and posed for pictures and bought them drinks. One especially, Hal Rutger of the Coast City *News-Record*, was an old friend of mine.

They looked at the overturned furniture. They looked at Merkel's black eye and at my torn shirt and bloody mouth. Then questions popped and camera bulbs flashed.

The Chief of Police held up a hand. "One at a time, boys. Give me a chance to tell you what happened. We got word that Sherman had sworn he'd kill Mayor Goodson and was on the way."

"Word from whom?" I cut in.

"Your own office. Albert Maurer and Enid Cooke. Seems you were going to beat Maurer up and then said you'd go after the Mayor instead and headed for here."

My teeth clamped over my cut lip. That story had enough truth in it to make whatever I said sound bad.

"My boys stopped him before he could reach the Mayor," Merkel was saying. "They had orders to handle him with kid gloves. I guess that was a mistake. They took him down here to cool off, but didn't search him. For a while he was quiet, then I came in and he pulled this gun of his and yelled he was going to kill Mayor Goodson." He pointed to his eye. "We had one hell of a time subduing him. If you ask me, he's off his nut."

"Can we quote you on that, Chief?"

"Sure thing. Sherman got caught red-handed in some crooked stuff, and when it hit the papers he went to pieces."

I yelled, "He's lying! They —"

I checked myself. My voice was too loud, too enraged. I sounded too much like the way they wanted me to sound — a man with so little control that in a fit of anger I had been on the way to murder the man who had removed me from my job. They were undermining me in every way possible.

More quietly I told the reporters that I was being framed and why — framed with the bribery story and now with my gun. Sure, I'd come to City Hall to tell Goodson what I thought of him, but my gun had been home. I hadn't touched it in months, perhaps in as much as a year. I'd get Goodson, all right, if it took me the rest of my life, but I wouldn't need a gun to do it. I'd expose him for the crook he was.

When I stopped talking, it was very still in the room. I dabbed at my bloody mouth and saw something like pity in the reporters' eyes. Whether they believed me or not was beside the point. They'd been made cynical on the city hall beat; they knew what little chance I had. And since they liked me, they were sorry for me.

Hal Rutger asked, "Chief, are you going to arrest him?"

"Well, now," Merkel massaged his jaw. "We can send him up for sixty days for armed assault, but I don't know if he'll be charged. You'll get a statement from the Mayor later."

The reporters were dismissed. When they were gone, Merkel whispered something to one of the detectives. The detective grabbed my arm and led me out of the room and up a flight of back stairs and through a door. I found myself outside the rear of the city hall.

"Scram, bum," he said and went back into the building.

4

Hal Rutger was waiting for me in the city hall plaza. I had thought he would. We'd been close friends for years. Like myself, he was a bachelor, but he made a career of it. Women fell for him and chased him as much as he chased them. He was also a first-rate newspaperman.

"I was pretty sure they wouldn't hold you," he said. "They don't dare bring you to trial where you'll be able to cross-examine Chief Merkel and his cops under oath."

"You mean you believe me?"

"I resent the question," he said. "Of course I do. All the way. But the rub's in that *all the way* part. Those who don't know you as well will have doubts. That means all the people in Coast City. They've become mighty cynical about politics, and with good reason. They're ready to take for granted that everybody is out for a fast buck. And there's nobody lower than a sanctimonious hypocrite. I'm afraid you're through, Paul."

"Like hell I am. I fought Goodson before I was on the Crime Commission. I'll fight him again."

"It's not the same. I'll do what I can for you, Paul. I'll slant my stories your way, but I'm not the publisher and I can go only so far. You're alone now, or almost alone. I spoke to the Citizens for a Clean City people — to Warrender and others. They're in a panic. They're afraid to go to bat for you because Goodson succeeded in making them wonder about you. He's turned the tables. All of a sudden he's the champion of good government and you're the one who's corrupt."

"All right then," I said, "I'll fight him alone."

Hal sighed. "With what? Goodson has all the weapons. He's used only two of them so far. He's isolated you, and he's set up an atmosphere where he can have you killed and get away with it. You've made one attempt on his life — anyway, that's the way he's made it appear. He can work it so that you're shot down by one of his cops while you're trying to murder him again. A little gaudy, but in the long run neat enough." Hal glanced sideways at me. "He wouldn't mind you being dead. I've an idea he's not sure Janie has stopped caring for you."

"That's been over almost three years."

"You sure, Paul?"

"Yes." I stuck a cigarette between my split lip. "I'm not running. If that's what you're getting at."

"You don't have to put it that way. But there's nothing left for you in Coast City. Even as a practicing lawyer you'll have no future here. The attempted bribery charges will be dropped if you simply go away. It's a big country, Paul. You can make a fresh start somewhere else."

"No," I said.

We crossed the plaza and stopped in front of the *News-Record* building.

Hal looked at his watch. "Thirty minutes to deadline. I'll give your side of it all I can in my story; but as you know, the publisher's a friend of Goodson's." He put a hand on my shoulder. "Good luck, Paul," he said, sounding as if I'd need all there was, and walked into the building.

My lip was still bleeding. I walked on holding my handkerchief pressed to my mouth. Before I did anything else, I'd have to doctor the cut and change my shirt. I hailed a cab.

My apartment was on the second floor of a modest brick building on a modest street. All there was to it, besides the bathroom and tiny kitchenette, was a combination bed and living room — adequate for a bachelor who did little or no entertaining. There was no foyer, so even before I had the door all the way open I saw Janie Goodson.

She was lying face down on the floor. One arm was outflung and her skirt was bunched up about her hips, showing the tautness of black garters against her white thighs.

5

I dropped down beside her and turned her over on her back. Her eyes were closed. Except that she was breathing raggedly through her mouth, she might have been merely asleep. She moaned as I carried her to the broad divan which served as my bed.

There was no visible wound, but my probing fingers discovered the lump at the base of her skull. She had been sapped by an expert, cleanly and without blood.

I fetched water and a washcloth from the bathroom and bathed her face. Her breathing became more regular; her lovely features relaxed. Her dress was still awry. I tugged the hem down to her knees. The backs of my hands brushed her warm bare thighs, and the blood drained from my fingers.

It was a long time since I had touched her at all.

Her eyelids fluttered, and then she was staring up at me with her dark, solemn eyes. Her arms moved.

They went around my neck and drew me down to her, and my bruised mouth was pressed against the sweetness of her mouth.

For one long moment I let myself go, then I stood up. I was breathing hard as I looked down at the beauty of her body, molded by the gray knitted dress.

"You haven't changed," she said.

I lit a cigarette. I said savagely, "Is this what you came for?"

Janie started to lift her head. Her face twisted with pain and she sank back. "Somebody knocked me out."

"So I gather. Who?"

"I don't know. I had to have a talk with you, Paul. Too many people were watching when we met on the city hall steps. It wouldn't have looked right now that you and Clyde are again enemies. That's why I acted so unfriendly. But then I came here to wait for you."

"How did you expect to get through a locked door?"

"Perhaps your door wasn't locked or perhaps a cleaning woman was here. I had nothing else to do. And the door wasn't locked, Paul. I suppose whoever was in here opened it with a passkey or some kind of tool. I simply walked in. He must have been in the bathroom. I heard somebody behind me and started to turn and then everything went black.

"That's nice," I said. "The Mayor's wife knocked out by one of the Mayor's cops."

"Was that who it was?"

"Probably. He came here to steal my gun. Evidently he didn't recognize you. You were just somebody he had to get rid of without being seen."

"Your gun?" She turned on her side to get a better view of me. "Paul, what happened to your mouth?"

Sitting in the armchair a dozen feet from her, I told her all of it.

"You're a fool," she said when I finished. "You've always been a fool. You could be a big man in town if you gave yourself the chance."

"Maybe I don't want to be that kind of big man."

"Don't you realize that Clyde can be absolutely ruthless?"

"Yes."

"Then what do you hope to gain?"

"It's the old story," I said. "You can't understand anybody who's not on the make. You turned me down because I was only a struggling lawyer and you married Goodson because he could give you a nice house and good clothes and make you a big shot socially. Was it worth it, Janie?"

"Of course it was," she said. "All my life I'd been poor. Now I have everything I want." She paused and a shadow crossed her face and she said, "Except . . ." and slowly sat up.

She swung her legs off the divan and stood up. "My head's splitting," she said, passing a hand over her brow, and she came over to where I sat.

There was a shimmering in her

dark eyes that I remembered well from the old days — a shimmering and that tightening of the cheeks that measured the intensity of her emotions. She dropped down near me. "Darling, listen to me. I couldn't stand anything happening to you."

I sat limp alongside her, resisting her by doing nothing at all, hating her and wanting her and deep within myself fighting her.

Once before after her marriage it had been like this. It was at a charity ball, the first time I had seen her in over a year, and in a strapless evening gown she had seemed so beautiful that looking at her was like a punch in the pit of my stomach. There wasn't a man in the place who could take his eyes off her. I avoided her until she asked me to dance, and after the number she led me out to the garden, and she had thrust herself at me. "Darling, I've been so lonely without you," she had said. I had assumed then that she'd had enough of Goodson and meant to leave him for me, but I soon discovered that that wasn't her idea at all. She told me she would come up to my apartment the following evening, but nothing else needed to be changed. "Don't be such a fool," she said because I couldn't see it her way. And I walked away from her. Because, much as I wanted her, I couldn't share her.

And now here again she had called me a fool, sitting near me. And I said coldly, "All right, Janie, what's the deal this time?"

"Deal?" Her mouth had been pressed against my cheek; she drew back her head. "You make it sound ugly. I don't know what you mean by deal. I simply want to save you from Clyde."

"Why?"

"Because I've never stopped loving you."

"What's that got to do with it if you prefer living with a man you don't love?"

She rose then. She stood with her side to me, her profile static, and looked down at her clasped hands as she spoke. "Paul, let's think about you for a minute. Just you alone. I can talk to Clyde. I have a great deal of influence with him. I can persuade him to make peace with you."

"It takes two to make peace."

She swung around to face me. "Paul, what do you want from him? I can get you almost anything within reason."

"We're still worlds apart," I said. "What I want is to see him and his pals behind bars."

"You'll never do it."

"I can keep trying."

She looked at me in disgust. Suddenly, the doorbell rang.

I answered the door. Enid Cooke and Hal Rutger were in the hall.

Hal said, "We met in front of the house," and he stepped over the threshold and saw Janie. He turned his head to me and said, "Is it wise at this time, Paul?" and then moved into the room.

"Hello, Hal," Janie said.

"Well, well, like old home week," he said. "The three of us together again. If you consider Enid my date, it will be like the old double dates when we were kids."

Enid stood silently, trim and blonde, and clung to her handbag with both hands. She stared at my face.

"Am I still bleeding?" I asked her.

She seemed embarrassed by my question and looked away. There was a kind of brittle silence in the room. Janie was picking up her mink stole from a chair. Hal held a lighter to his cigarette.

I went into the bathroom. The mirror showed me something brighter than blood on my face. The smear of Janie's lipstick was quite definite on my cheek.

Savagely I scrubbed it off.

When I returned to the room, Hal and Janie stood together at a window speaking in undertones so that Enid, who hadn't stirred from the entrance door, wouldn't overhear them. I could imagine what he was telling her — that matters for me would go from bad to worse if her husband were to find out she had been there. And seeing them together, I thought of the good times we had had when we were kids. Janie and Hal and I and the rest of the gang on the shabby street. Of us all, Janie was the one who had risen farthest — anyway, in the eyes of the world.

She was coming toward me now, carrying her mink stole, saying, "Paul, please bear in mind what I told you. If you want me to talk to Clyde . . ."

"I want you to leave me alone," I said.

She shrugged and continued to the door. Enid stepped aside to let her go by. Hal told me, "I'll grab a lift with Janie downtown," and walked after her.

I moved to the window. An expensive convertible was parked in front of the house; it would be Janie's. I watched her and Hal come out of the building together, talking urgently. About me, no doubt. About how to protect me from my own pig-headedness. I wished to hell they would let me solve my own problems.

"I suppose," Enid said, "making love to that woman was more important than saving your records."

I had forgotten she was in the apartment. I turned to her. "You're my business secretary, not my social secretary."

She flushed. "I'm nobody's secretary now. Don't forget that my job ended with yours this morning."

"I'm also remembering that the police were notified I'd threatened to kill the Mayor."

"Paul, do you really think I did it? Albert Maurer called them as soon as you left the office this morning. I heard him use my name; he said I'd also heard you. Of course it was a lie. I mean" — she fidgetted — "well, you didn't really say you were going to kill him."

If not even Enid was sure of me, what could I expect from anybody else? I dropped on the divan and put my head in my hands. I was suddenly very tired.

"What's this about the records?" I asked with little interest.

"That's what I came here to tell you. The police have taken over the office and won't let anybody near the files."

"It doesn't matter much. If the records were important, I would have done something about them when I had the chance."

"I see," she said. "You're giving up. Hal Rutger told me you weren't."

"No, I'm not giving up. But most of the stuff in the files was about small fry. Only Goodson counts now, and we'd hardly started the job on him. I would have had to begin almost from scratch anyway."

Enid had moved to my side. "You can count on me, Paul."

"You're a swell kid, Enid," I said and reached out and pressed her shoulder.

She cried, "Leave me alone!" and whirled and ran out of the apartment.

I didn't get it at all.

6

In the evening a special meeting of the executive board of Citizens for a Clean City was held in Peter B. Warrender's bank. I stated my case to the dozen non-committal faces. I said I had worked with them for good government; they knew me well and had no reason not to trust me. They were among the leading business and professional men in town, and with their help I could resume my activity to clean up the city.

When I was through, Warrender made one of his long-winded speeches. He stated that probably everything I had said was true, but my effectiveness with the public had been destroyed until I could prove my innocence beyond doubt. Besides, I had indicated irresponsibility by rushing to city hall with a gun in my pocket and then getting into a fight with the police. Here again my version might be the true one, but possibly not. Citizens for a Clean City couldn't put itself out on a limb. He stopped talking.

The others voiced substantially the same sentiment.

"Thank you, gentlemen," I said bitterly and got out of there.

Twenty minutes later I came within an inch of being murdered.

I was approaching my apartment building on that quiet street when a small explosion roused me from my bleak thoughts. My first reaction was that a car moving slowly toward me was backfiring. Again there was that barking explosion, and at the same time my hat was tugged as if by an invisible hand.

I was being shot at. The gunman was deep in the shadows of a doorway across the street while I was a clear target in the glare of a street lamp. And he was getting the range.

The building entrance was a good thirty feet away, and he would expect me to head for it. Crouching, I ran the other way.

There was no third shot. Instead somebody called urgently, "Paul!" I looked up and a long, sleek convertible, with Janie behind the wheel, slid to the curb. It was a shield between me and the gunman.

The right door was toward me, waiting open for me. I dove for it. Janie put the car into motion before I was all the way inside. We roared away.

"My God, Paul!" she said. "I told you I was afraid of something like this."

I examined my hat. The crown had a frayed spot where the bullet had nicked it. "How'd you happen to be at the right spot at the right time?"

"I was waiting for you. Paul, seeing you again this morning, kissing you, I realized that I couldn't go on with Clyde. I never liked him very much, and I never stopped loving you."

She seemed to mean it. I looked at her face shadowed in blurred planes by the dashboard light. She was wearing a tweed skirt and a white sweater that emphasized her breasts.

"I'll do anything you want," she went on. "I'll go away with you."

It was no longer that simple. Since this morning there was nobody I could believe or trust.

"Haven't you anything to say?" she asked.

"You caught me at the wrong time."

She glanced sidelong at me. "Is it your secretary, Enid Cooke?"

"What about her?"

"Don't tell me you don't know she's carrying the torch for you?"

"Enid? That's ridiculous."

"Darling, you don't appreciate your sex appeal. Hal told me she's in love with you, and I could see for myself by the way she reacted when she found me in your apartment and saw my lipstick on your face."

I understood now why Enid had run out of my apartment. She was a very nice girl. I was sorry.

"There's never been anybody but you," I said.

Janie smiled and stepped harder on the gas. We were on the shore road and I could hear the roar of the ocean and there was a glimpse of gray water under bright moonlight.

"Where are we going?" I asked.

"I've a bathhouse nearby. Nobody would think of looking for you there."

"You expect me to hide?"

"Well, you can't go home just yet, can you? Whoever shot at you might be waiting for you. You ought to stay away at least until daylight."

She had something there.

Presently she swung the convertible onto a narrow oiled road running through sand. Close to the shore she pulled up beside a small clapboard cabin. Almost disdainfully, she had referred to it as a bathhouse, but when we were inside I found it had electric and plumbing and a fireplace and was furnished better than the slum flat in which she'd been raised.

I'd hardly followed her over the threshold when she was in my arms. "Paul!" she said, clinging to me.

I said, "You'll get a divorce and then we'll be married."

"Yes, yes. But let's not talk now."

It was not like this morning or any time since her marriage. There was no longer any question of sharing her. From now on she would be all mine, and here tonight we finally and forever belonged to each other. Together we moved to the daybed against the wall, stumbling a little on the way, and then my thoughts blurred with my need of her and the overwhelming beauty of her body.

7

I had built a fire in the fireplace, and we lay stretched out in front of it on a blanket. Outside the surf roared and crashed, while in the cabin there was quiet.

She said, "In a little while I'll go home and —"

"Not your home any more, Janie."

She kissed me. "From now on my home is wherever you are. But I'll have to get my things — at least pack a bag. Then we'll go far away from Coast City."

"No," I said. "We're not running."

"Darling, are you going to start that again? You were almost killed tonight. Clyde will have so much more reason to want you dead when he finds out about this."

"I'm not running, Janie."

For a while she lay silent with her head on my shoulder. Then she said, "Once when I was hanging up one of Clyde's suits I found a small memo book. It was full of names and figures. I realized what they meant. They were records of his — well, his transactions. I suppose he has to keep some kind of record."

I stirred. "In his handwriting."

"Yes. Written in the green ink he uses. Paul, if you had that book, would you be safe from him?"

"It will give me leads," I said. "Maybe even enough evidence to present to the grand jury, and from there on I'll have plenty of help. Have you got it?"

"No, but I'm sure it's somewhere in the house. He wouldn't let it be far from him. I'll go at once to look for it." She paused. "I hate to do this to him because he's been kind to me. But he'll destroy you if you don't destroy him first, so I have to make the choice."

"It will take time to do the job. Weeks and months."

"I know. I'll stay with my parents until we're both free." She rose from the blanket. "I'd better go now if I expect to be back tonight."

For another minute I lingered there by the fire, watching her dress. Then I got into my own clothes and went out with her to her car.

"If he's home, I'll have to wait until he's asleep before I start searching," she told me. "Don't worry if it's hours before I return."

We kissed for a long time. Then she drove off.

I didn't go back into the cabin to wait. The night was mild and the moon was bright. I walked along the beach, remembering what had just happened, and it was as if I could still feel the wild responsiveness of her flesh. It would be hard to keep away from her until her divorce, but it would be necessary for several reasons.

But I could wait. I had waited a long time. I sat on a small sand dune and watched the ocean.

When my cigarette was gone, I looked at my watch. Slightly less than an hour had passed since she had left. It was a fifteen-minute drive to her house — or rather to the Mayor's mansion which had been her house until tonight. Still plenty of time, but I started back.

A shot sounded above the roar of the surf.

8

For a moment I thought I was again being shot at. I dropped down on the sand. Then there were more shots, three or four overlapping, and I realized that they were some distance off. I jumped up and ran on to the cabin. The soft sand made my movements as maddeningly slow as in a nightmare.

I rounded a dune and saw several hundred feet away the lights of the cabin and the glare of car headlights. The headlights swept in a turn and I heard an engine being gunned. The car receded, disappeared, but Janie's convertible was there beside the cabin. It stood dark and empty, and it looked terrifyingly forlorn.

I burst into the cabin, and it was like this morning all over when I had entered my apartment and had found Janie motionless on the floor. Only now she would never awaken. Her nose was gone where one of the bullets had smashed through.

She lay on her back, her torso curiously twisted, one hand almost in the glowing embers of the fire. I hardly had the strength to move the short distance to her. I dropped to the floor beside her and lifted her hand. The coldness of death was already on her flesh.

I don't know how long I sat there, holding that lifeless hand. There were other bullets in her. I could see the hole in the white sweater at the swell of her right breast. There was no blood on the sweater. She had already been dead when that bullet entered.

He had pointed the gun at her and emptied it into her. He had followed her here, and had known that I had been here with her, and that had turned him into a madman.

I roused then and stood up and looked around for a sign, for evidence. All I saw was evidence pointing to me. There was my hat on the table. There were the butts of the cigarettes I had smoked; my dried saliva on the tips would enable the police laboratory to determine the blood type of the smoker. And there were my fingerprints all over the place.

I could do nothing for her. All that was left was for me to try to save myself.

I gathered up the cigarette stubs and put them into the heart of what remained of the fire. I had to step over her body to do so, and that was pretty bad. Then as I wiped with my pocket handkerchief everything I could have touched, I tried not to look at her lying so still and cold on the floor.

Moving across the room, I kicked something. Stupidly I stood staring down at her handbag on the floor. I knew there was something important I had to remember, but my brain was sluggish with grief and shock. I went on to the pine table and wiped the top and suddenly it hit me.

She had gone for Goodson's memo book. If she had returned so soon, it must mean that she had found it quicker than expected.

It was in her handbag, all right, stuck in between a wallet and a compact. I leafed through the pages, glanced at names and figures in green ink. Ruining Goodson politically seemed almost unimportant now.

Outside I heard a car.

I rushed to the window. In moonlight I could see a white sedan turning in from the paved road.

State police cars were white! The killer must have known I was nearby and would be back; he would be anxious to have me caught on the scene. He had put in an anonymous call to the state police as soon as he had reached a phone, and now here they were. I flung open the door.

I almost left my hat on the table. I went back for it, and that brief delay proved disastrous. By the time I was again outside, the approaching headlights were close enough to pick me out of the darkness, to let the men in the car get a good look at me.

I dashed around the corner of the cabin. Somebody shouted an order to halt. I ran out into the night.

9

It took a lot of scratching on the window to wake Enid Cooke. I had to be as quiet as possible about it so as not to wake her parents and her two younger brothers, who would be asleep in other parts of the house.

Luckily this was a one-story, ranch-type structure hugging the ground, so that, standing, I could see into her room. Moonlight flowing in through the two casement windows revealed her blonde head shifting on the pillow. I whispered her name through the window screen.

She turned on her side. "Who's there?" she asked, in a startled tone.

"It's Paul Sherman. Can you come to the window?"

She slipped out of bed. Her nightgown looked no more substantial than the moonbeams. She came close to the window and peered at my face on the other side of the screen.

"What is it, Paul?" she whispered.

"I'm in trouble. I need your help."

"I'll be right out."

I moved away from the window to the deep shadows along the garage. This was a new housing development at the outskirts of the town; it was surrounded by other houses exactly like Enid's. Everybody in them seemed asleep. I looked at my watch. Twenty after two. Janie had been dead an hour and a half.

Enid appeared in housecoat and slippers. Softly I called to her, and when she reached me she gripped my arm.

"You're hiding from Mayor Goodson," she whispered.

"I'm hiding all right. Listen."

I told her everything that had happened.

She stood very still beside me listening, not speaking until I had finished. Then she said, "And now because there's nobody else, you come to me."

"Do you want me to go?"

"No, Paul. I'll help you any way you want me to. Can they prove you were there with her?"

"That depends on how good a look the state troopers had of me and if there's any evidence pointing to me in the cabin. Hal Rutger can find out; as a newspaperman he'll have an inside track. But I can't risk going to his place. It's known he's my close friend and the police might be watching him."

"All right," she said. "Do you want me to go at once?"

"If you don't mind." I put my hand on her shoulder. "Enid, I didn't know you cared for me."

This time she didn't pull away from me. She looked at my hand on her shoulder. "Would it have made any difference if you had known?" she said woodenly.

"I suppose not. I loved Janie."

"You and how many others?" she asked. Her voice was too loud amid all those houses; she lowered it, but there was a quiver in it. "You and whatever man she wanted to sleep with."

"Enid, I won't let you talk like that about her."

She laughed, a laugh without humor. "Don't tell me you thought you were the only one?"

"What do you mean?"

"It was an open scandal in town. Everybody knew about how the Mayor's wife carried on — everybody but her husband. And, it seems, you."

My hand dropped from her. I leaned against the side of the garage.

"Are you sure, Enid?"

"Of course I'm sure. Let me tell you."

Standing there in the shadows, she told me. And I believed her because it made sense. Nothing else made sense.

"I see," I said, and for a little while at least I didn't care if I lived or died.

She stood close to me. "I'm sorry, Paul. Perhaps I should have kept my mouth shut."

"No. It's better this way." I

reached into my pocket for a cigarette, forgetting that I had smoked my last while waiting on the beach for Janie to return. I said, "I've changed my message for Hal. Tell him I can prove who killed Janie."

"Can you?" she asked quietly. She had moved half a dozen feet away from me and stood a barely distinguishable shape against the garage wall.

"Tell Hal there's no doubt. I can prove it. Tell him to meet me in Mayor Goodson's house as soon as he can get there."

"The Mayor's house?"

"That's right. I'll have the evidence with me. And, Enid, you come with him."

She didn't question that. She had no more to ask or to say. She moved toward the house, and I watched her until she was out of sight.

10

Dawn was not far off, but in that colonial house on a hill Mayor Goodson had not yet gone to bed. From behind bushes I had watched him return home about an hour ago, coming, I assumed, from that cabin where he had been shown his wife's body. Light had gone on in the wing that housed his study. I had crept close to the French doors that opened on a terrace and watched his chubby body slumped in a chair. For that entire hour he had hardly moved.

I could feel almost sorry for him now.

I fingered his little memo book in my pocket. Since leaving Enid tonight, I'd had plenty of time to study it. There wasn't, after all, much that could be done with it. Goodson had used a kind of shorthand; those who knew the score, like myself, could figure some of it out, but it wouldn't be concrete evidence. Its only use would be in a step by step investigation to build up the case against him. Yesterday I would have considered that extremely valuable. Now it no longer seemed important.

I heard a car stop on the street below. I slipped across the lawn to the blacktop driveway and waited there for Hal Rutger and Enid Cooke to come up to me.

Hal whispered, "Have you really got something, Paul?"

"Yes."

"It better be good. The cops are after you. A state trooper recognized you as the guy who ran out of the cabin. Enid gave me your story. I believe it, but who else will?"

"They'll believe it," I said. "Let's go."

I started across the lawn.

Hal caught up to me. "The Mayor, huh? It figures."

"Does it?" I said, and stumbled against him. I threw my arms about him to save myself from falling.

He shoved me away from him. For a moment we stood facing each other with Enid looking on. Dawn was coming up and I could see his big brown eyes wide and solemn. I grinned mirthlessly and moved on.

I led the way up on the terrace and shoved open the French door and entered the study. Hal and Enid were right behind me.

Goodson lifted his head. His face had gone to pieces; it was all loose flesh. He blinked once and then came out of his chair.

"Hold it," I said. "I didn't kill her."

He checked himself, perhaps not so much because of what I had said as because for the first time he became aware of the others in the room.

"The police saw you," he said.

"True enough." I stepped sideways, putting myself behind Hal. "But I can prove Hal Rutger did it."

A clock in the study ticked loudly.

Hal looked at me over his shoulder. "Is this a gag, Paul?"

"In a way," I admitted. "To get you here with your gun. I stumbled against you a minute ago on purpose. I felt it in your pocket."

Hal pushed his hand into his jacket pocket. "So what? I came here to meet a murderer, either you or Goodson. I figured it might come in handy."

Goodson said, "I don't understand."

"You didn't and I didn't," I told him. "Janie fooled us both. Not you so much; she married you for your money and position. But she found her love-life elsewhere. With a number of men. We'll never know with whom and how many. But mostly with Hal. We two weren't the only ones, Goodson, who were crazy in love with her."

Goodson stared, his mouth a white line.

"Enid told me tonight, about the others and especially about Hal. He'd boasted to her about his conquest of the Mayor's beautiful wife. And I believed it because it completed the pattern. Last night somebody shot at me, tried to kill me. My first thought was that it was you, Goodson, or a hired killer sent by you."

"I would have been out of my mind."

I nodded. "That occurred to me when I had a chance to think it over. With all this bad feeling between us, the public would have realized that you'd had me killed. You would have been finished politically. We were out to get each other, but neither of us could afford to do it that way. If not you, then who? It wasn't until Janie had been murdered and I learned about her and Hal that the answer came up."

Hal shifted in a half-turn so that he could face me. I remained close to him.

"You didn't mind sharing her with her husband and minor lovers," I told him. "You had her and that satisfied you. But all along you were afraid of me. I suppose I was the one she really loved; you and the others were only substitutes. You knew that. You knew I was the one who could take her away from you. And when you walked in on us in my apartment yesterday morning and saw her lipstick on my cheek, you got in a panic. You had to eliminate me. So that night you tried to kill me. You failed and I drove off with Janie. You had a good idea where we'd go; you must have spent many an hour in that cabin with her. You saw us" — my voice shook a little — "and you heard her say she would divorce Goodson and marry me. You brooded about it while she was gone to get the memo book, and when she returned you emptied your gun into her."

I paused and then said, "That gun in your pocket, Hal. When Enid gave you my message and I knew who the murderer was and had evidence, you had to bring a gun. It's probably the only one you have, and you decided you might need it if it turned out that I actually could prove your guilt. You'd want to stop me. But you can't stop the three of us. You brought our evidence, Hal."

Goodson moved then. He went over to the phone to call the police.

The gun came out of Hal's pocket. He said, "Stay away from that phone." His mouth twisted. "How are you going to prove this gun shot Janie when I get rid of it?"

I dove at him. I had every move planned in advance. His gun was high, pointed at Goodson, and I dove low under it. My shoulders hit him above the knees. He slammed over backward.

His right arm flailed, trying to get the gun to bear on me. I twisted his wrist with one hand and with the other hand tore the gun from his fingers. I hurled it across the floor.

Goodson was bending over for the gun when I stood up. He straightened and his face was the consistency and color of dough.

Both Hal and Enid screamed. Hal stopped screaming after the first shot. Deliberately Goodson put two more bullets into him. Then listlessly he moved to the phone.

I turned and saw Enid sagging and held her trembling body in my arms. Neither of us looked at the body.

Again I could hear the clock tick. And then there was Goodson's voice saying tonelessly to the police, "This is Clyde Goodson. I've just killed my wife's murderer."

We went out on the terrace, Enid and I, to wait for the police. She said, "You planned it this way."

"I suppose so."

"You didn't have to wait till he took the gun out of his pocket. And you didn't have to throw it to Goodson. You knew what would happen."

"I didn't know, but I thought it might." I watched the sky turn pink with dawn. "After all, he was her husband," I said.

Enid's shoulder was against mine. I thought of what a very nice girl she was.

I hadn't known many nice people.

The Follower

BY

HUNT COLLINS

She swore a man followed her home every night. But each time her husband investigated, there just wasn't anyone there.

THE MAN followed her home again that night.

She caught a quick glimpse of him as she stepped off the bus, and when she turned her head to look behind her, he ducked into the heavy shadows of the big oak on the corner.

It was still not dark at this hour of the evening, but Autumn was rapidly drawing to a close, and she knew darkness would come earlier in the next few weeks. She walked fast in the gathering dusk, listening to the small click of her heels against the pavement, hearing the footsteps behind her like an echoing whisper. It was five blocks to her house from the bus stop, five lonely blocks of weed-grown lots, of immense trees that cast huge pockets of shadow.

Tonight, she almost ran the last two blocks, listening to the padded footsteps speeding up behind her as she quickened her pace.

She threw open the door, slammed it shut when she was inside, and then leaned her back against it, the palms of her hands moist. A shudder trickled down her spine like a cold drop of water. She felt the reassuring sturdiness of the door behind her, sighed deeply, and walked into the living room so bright and warm.

"That you, Ella?" Bob called from the den.

"Yes, darling." She draped her topcoat over the arm of a chair, dropped her gloves and purse onto the seat. She stopped before the long mirror over the couch, fluffed her hair, and then walked into the den.

Bob looked up from his desk, and she walked to him and kissed him lightly on the cheek.

"Hey now, that's a hell of a greeting for a man," he complained.

He pulled her down onto his lap, kissed her on the mouth, and then pulled away and looked at her curiously. "Something wrong, hon?" he asked.

"No, nothing," she said quickly. She watched his brows pull together into a pucker, shading the intense blue of his eyes. "Well, yes, Bob, there is something. I . . . you'll think I'm foolish, but . . ."

"The Shadow again?"

She stood up abruptly. "Don't joke about it, Bob!"

"I'm sorry, Ella. What happened this time?"

"He . . . he was there again."

"At the bus stop?"

"Yes."

"And?"

"He followed me again. He . . . he was right behind me all the way."

"All the way to the house?"

"Yes."

Bob shoved his chair back, and swung his legs from beneath the desk. He walked past Ella and into the living room. He stood near the window, spreading the slats of the blind apart with his fingers. Ella watched him nervously.

"I don't see anyone out there," he said over his shoulder.

"You don't expect him to stand out there all night, do you?"

Bob sighed deeply, releasing the slats. "No, I suppose not."

"Bob, we've got to do something about him. It'll be getting dark earlier the next few weeks and I'm . . . I'm afraid of what he might do."

"Ella," Bob said, "don't be silly, honey."

"What's so silly about it? I'm young and . . . well, fairly attractive, and . . ."

"You're beautiful," he corrected. He went to her and took both her hands in his. "Honey, I'd follow you home myself."

"Well, then, there is a real danger, Bob. Can't you see there is?"

"Ella, if I thought there was . . ." He stopped, suddenly releasing her hands. "But where *is* this mystery man of yours? The first night you told me about him, I rushed right out and scoured the neighborhood. There wasn't a soul in sight, unless you want to count old Mr. Jaeger next door."

"This man isn't Mr. Jaeger."

"All right, honey," he said earnestly, " butwho is he? *Where* is he? I've met you at the bus stop three times since you claim he . . ."

"Claim? Don't you believe me, Bob?"

"Of course I believe you. I shouldn't have said 'claim.' What I meant was . . . well, each time I met you at the bus, I didn't see anyone lurking around, or anyone who even looked mildly suspicious."

"That doesn't mean anything. Maybe he saw you waiting there and just went away."

"Maybe. But the last time I met you, I got there about three seconds before the bus pulled in. He certainly wouldn't have had enough time to spot me and hightail it. Not unless he lives in the big apartment near the bus stop. Honey . . ."

"Maybe he just wasn't there that night. You know he's not there every night."

"Honey," Bob said, "can't you just forget him? Can't you . . ."

"How can I?" she wailed. "How can I forget him when I hear him behind me? Bob, he frightens me to death. And when I think of it getting dark soon . . ."

"Baby, baby," he said gently. He took her in his arms. "Come on now, none of that. Look, as soon as it starts getting dark, I'll meet you at the bus every night. How's that?"

"What about your work? You have so much to do at night," she said hesitantly.

"Never mind my work. We'll try meeting you instead, okay? Maybe The Shadow will just . . ."

"You're joking again," she said.

"But not about meeting you. I'll be there every night. Does that make you feel better?" He lifted her chin with his bent forefinger. "Does it?"

"Yes," she answered in a small voice.

"Fine. Let's eat. I'm starved."

Winter came quickly, and with it the early darkness she had been dreading. Bob met her at the bus stop every night, and they chatted on the long five-block walk to their home.

They saw no one.

The lot-straddled streets were deserted, and the only footfalls they heard were their own. She began to feel extremely foolish about the whole matter now, especially when Bob joked about it in his easy way. But at the same time, she could not ignore her earlier fears. Bob did not complain. He met her religiously every evening, even though he lost valuable working time which he had to make up later in the night. She thought of this often, and was tempted several times to tell him to forget all about it.

But one week stretched into another, and she could not forget the man or the furtive way he had ducked out of sight whenever she turned to look at him. She still remembered the rasping scrape of his shoes against the pavement, and the terror that had gripped her, walking the lonely stretch of streets. She was still frightened, and she didn't ask Bob to stop meeting her.

They never spoke of her fears any more. As the weeks expanded into a month, and then two months, Bob's meeting her became something of a ritual, a thing of courtship that she looked forward to each night. She almost hoped that he had forgotten exactly *why* he was meeting her, that he looked forward to their brisk evening walk as much as she did.

It wasn't until January that anything happened.

Bob called her at the office one day. The sky was grey with the promise of snow, banks of foreboding clouds piled against the horizon. When she heard his voice, it relieved her melancholy mood almost instantly.

"Darling," she said, "what a surprise!"

"Hello, honey," he said, "how's it going?"

"A little dreary, but otherwise fine." She paused, wondering suddenly why he'd called. "Is anything wrong, Bob?"

"Well, no, not exactly. In fact, this may really turn into something good."

"What, Bob?"

"I've got to see the vice president of Thomas Paul and Sons tonight. They're thinking of taking their account to us."

"Why, that's wonderful!"

"Sure, if we can swing it. That's why I called, honey."

"Why?"

"I have to go there directly from the office. I won't be able to meet you at the bus."

A long silence clutched the line.

"Oh," she said at last.

"Honey, you're not going to get silly on me again, are you? Really, Ella, there's nothing to be afraid of. You don't think I'd leave you alone if there was, do you?"

"No," she said.

"And this can be a big thing, hon, honestly. If I can work this switch, I'll really be . . ."

"I know, I know," she said quickly.

"And you don't mind?"

"No. Of course not, Bob. You . . . you go ahead and do what you have to do." She was thinking of the empty streets, the dark lots, the huge trees. "I . . . I'll manage."

"You're sure now, hon? Just say the word and I'll . . ."

"No, Bob, I'll be all right."

"You're positive?"

"Yes. Yes."

"I won't be home too late," he said, "but don't hold supper for me."

"All right."

"Wish me luck."

"Good luck, darling."

"Goodbye, honey."

" 'Bye."

She heard a click on the line, but she held the receiver to her ear long after his voice had gone.

When she got off the bus that night, she saw the man standing on the corner. He was waiting.

A stab of panic fluttered into her throat, and she started to turn, wanting to step onto the bus again. But the doors slammed shut behind her, and she moved away rapidly as the gears ground and the bus rumbled off down the street. She looked nervously toward the big apartment house across the street, saw the man dodge into the shadows of the oak again. She wet her lips and started walking, praying she would meet someone.

The streets were deserted.

Her own heels clacked on the pavement, and behind her she could hear the steady scrape of the man's shoes. Her hands began to tremble, and she clenched them together to keep them steady. She swallowed the aching terror in her throat, and continued to walk, hearing the footsteps quicken behind her.

She was entering a stretch of ground flanked by large, solid trees. Their branches were bare, but they were heavy and they arched over the sidewalk, blotting out whatever moonlight there was. She quickened her pace, listening to the sound of her heels and the thunder of her own heart in her ears.

Tears sprang into her eyes and coursed down her cheeks. She bit her lower lip until she tasted the salty flow of blood in her mouth. The footsteps were still behind her.

She stopped suddenly, and the follower stopped.

There was only the darkness, and the silence, and the deep terror.

She began walking again, straining her ears until she heard the sullen shuffle behind her. Had he come closer? Didn't his footsteps sound closer?

She stopped again, whirled abruptly, and shouted, "Don't come near me!"

She heard the echo of her own voice on the deserted street. She sobbed wildly, staring into the darkness.

"Go away! Go away, or I'll scream!"

There was no answer. She felt him waiting there in the darkness, silently watching.

"*Go away!*" she shrieked. And then the scream bubbled onto her lips, high and piercing. She listened to it, shocked until she realized it was coming from her own throat. She heard the footsteps start again, heard them break into a fast run. She dropped to the pavement, her shoulders heaving, a wash of relief flooding her body. She heard more footsteps, running, and she almost screamed aloud again until she heard a voice she recognized.

"Mrs. Brant? Is that you, Mrs. Brant?"

She tried to speak, but her voice was smothered with sobs. She nodded her head dumbly, waited until Mr. Jaeger drew up alongside her.

"Mrs. Brant, are you all right?"

She nodded again, her face buried in her hands. She felt extremely childish, sitting in the middle of the pavement, sobbing like this before a strange old man.

"Come on, now, I'll take you home." His voice was kind, but puzzled. He helped her to her feet, and she looked down the long, dark street once more before they turned toward her house.

It was empty.

Mr. Jaeger and his wife sat with her until Bob came home. When he walked into the living room and saw them there, he rushed to Ella immediately.

"What's wrong?" he asked. "What happened?"

His hands were cold from the outdoors when he took her in his arms. "Ella, darling, darling, what's happened?"

"I found her sitting in the middle of the sidewalk," Mr. Jaeger put in. "Just sitting there and crying. Down by the empty lots. You know."

"Did you see anyone?" Bob asked quickly.

"Why, no. Just her. I heard her scream, and so I came running. I didn't see anyone." Mr. Jaeger shook his head. "Just her sitting there."

Bob sighed deeply and held her close. "Thank you very much, Mr. Jaeger," he said. "I really appreciate this."

"Glad to be of help," Mr. Jaeger said. "Come on, Martha, we'd best be getting to bed."

They said goodnight, and Bob closed the door firmly behind them. He passed a hand over his hair then, took off his coat, and asked wearily. "All right, honey, what happened?"

"The . . . the man. He followed me again. I . . . Bob, please, Bob."

"What man? What man are you talking about?"

"The one near the bus. You know, Bob. The one who . . ."

He went to her and took her in his arms. "Darling," he said gently, "there is no man near the bus."

She pulled out of his arms and looked up at him. "But . . . but there is! He followed me. Bob, he did. He was behind me. I heard him. Bob, for God's sake . . ."

"Listen to me, darling," he said, "please listen to me. This . . . this man of yours. He . . . he's just an . . . an exaggeration. The darkness, and the shadows, they all combine to make you think someone is there when . . ."

She began sobbing suddenly. "Bob, please believe me. If *you* don't believe me, I don't know what I'll do. There was someone. He followed me, Bob. I screamed, and he ran away."

"Then why didn't Mr. Jaeger see him, honey?"

"He ran away before Mr. Jaeger came." She stared at him searchingly. "Bob, you don't think I'm imagining all this!"

Their eyes met for an instant, and she saw tenderness on his face, but it was mixed with disbelief.

"*Bob, there was a man!*"

He took her in his arms again, and gently stroked her hair. "When I was a kid, honey, I was afraid to go down into the basement of our house. One day, my mother left me alone. I went up and down those cellar steps twenty-three times until I proved to myself there was nothing there to fear."

"Bob . . ."

"Ella, I want you to do me a favor."

"What? What is it, Bob?"

"Tell me you'll try walking home alone for a few days. Just to . . ."

"No!" she flared. "How could I? Bob, I . . . I . . ."

"Just for a few days. I want you to see for yourself that there's no one following you. After that, if you still insist . . . well, we'll see then. Promise me that, will you, darling?"

"Bob," she murmured, "please don't make me. Please, Bob. Please."

"We'll let you work this out yourself. That's the best way. What do you say, Ella, will you try it?"

She shook her head, as if trying to clear it. "Bob, you don't understand. You just don't understand." She kept shaking her head, holding back the frustrated tears.

"Will you try it?"

She took a deep breath.

"Will you?" he repeated.

She looked up into his face and saw the grim resolution there. She knew that he would never understand, and the knowledge crushed her defiance and left her suddenly lonely.

"All right," she said wearily. "All right, Bob."

The man was there again at the bus stop the next night.

She heard his footsteps as she began walking down the lonely, deserted stretch of pavement. When she entered the tree-flanked area, he was close behind her.

She quickened her steps, and she heard him walking faster, too. Closer.

For an instant, she wondered if the man wasn't a part of her imagination, wondered if Bob hadn't been right all along.

And then the hand clamped down over her mouth, stifling any scream, any sound she might have made. The hand was rough and large, and the pressure on her lips hurt. She felt herself being dragged into the bushes, her skirt catching and tearing on the twisted brambles. His hand sought the open throat of her blouse beneath the coat, moved swiftly, expertly.

She tried to scream then.

Her lips parted, but he hit her with his fist, and the scream became a muted, futile sob as he pulled her to the ground.

CRIME CAVALCADE

BY VINCENT H. GADDIS

Baby-Sitting Burglar

Police in Houston, Tex., are looking for a burglar who temporarily turned baby-sitter. After breaking into an apartment, the intruder noticed seven-month-old Denise Bernard in her crib. The Bernards keep a bottle filled with water handy every night, to quiet Denise if she becomes fretful. Apparently afraid that the infant might cry, the burglar gave her the bottle. He left with a billfold containing $40.

Sure Fire Bet

Lydel Sims, Memphis, Tenn., reports that you can't lose if you bet with the right people. Last November Sims lost an election bet with a local minister and paid off by check. The check has never been cashed. He wrote "gambling debt" on its face.

Self Arrest

In Peoria, Ill., Charles Lawson appeared in city court to pay a fine for driving through a stop sign. Judge Harold Arnold noticed that there was no arresting officer with him. Lawson then explained that he had arrested himself, because he was "worried" about his own carelessness. Arnold dismissed the case.

Including the Sink

Charles Crane, a Baltimore, Md., real estate dealer, started out with a $7500 house and ended up with a wooden shell. Shortly after purchasing the house, he discovered it was being stripped by vandals, piece by piece. First the radiators were stolen. Then came the furnace, plumbing fixtures and pipes, and the interior woodwork. Finally the thieves walked off with the kitchen sink. Disgusted, Crane hired a wrecking crew to tear down the house.

Strange Music

Police in Newark, N. J., are certain that the youth who dropped a violin case and fled, as officers broke up a street fight, was not taking music lessons. The case contained a 14-inch butcher knife, a two-and-a-half foot Japanese bayonet, and a length of lead pipe.

Third Degree

The term "third degree" as applied to police methods was believed coined by Major Richard Sylvester, superintendent of police in Washington, D. C., about the year 1911. Sylvester, who derived the term from Free-Masonry, said the law administers the first degree when a person is arrested, the second when the prisoner is placed in confinement, and the third when he is questioned. The term, of course, usually refers to the use of violent methods to extort a confession. However the Supreme Court has declared several times that confessions obtained under duress are not proper evidence.

Family Affair

When police in Hamilton, Ont., arrested Conley Clemens for failure to have a driver's license, they started a chain reaction. It all happened in less than two hours. Clemens' aunt went to the police station to learn where Conley was, and was arrested for drunkenness. His mother showed up next and was locked up for being disorderly and abusive. Finally his father appeared, and he was promptly jailed for failure to register the car.

Auto Assault

Paul Atkinson, 28, of Milwaukee, Wis., has been freed on a $500 bond after being charged with assaulting a parked automobile. Police said he went to work on the car with a hammer after he found it in his favorite parking place. According to the report of the officer investigating the offense, he put 28 dents in the body of the car, cracked the windshield and windows, broke the tail lights and let the air out of the rear tires.

Master Masks

Montreal police are using masks in a new effort to identify criminal suspects. The masks, made of plaster of Paris, combine almost every type of facial feature, and are used to assist witnesses to identify persons wanted for serious crimes if photographs of the suspects cannot be found in the department's rogues' gallery. Basic features differ in each of the seven masks.

Sullen Safe Crackers

Burglars in Knoxville, Tenn., blew their tops after they finally battered open a safe in a factory office and found it empty. They left a note on the desk reading: "Why didn't you leave some money in this thing?" Then they set fire to some sawdust in the boiler room, filling the building with smoke.

Roller Skate Robbery

Mrs. Virginia Charles told police in Los Angeles, Calif., that two teen-age girls swooped down on her from behind, seized her purse containing $50, and disappeared into the darkness. The girls were on roller skates.

I'm Getting Out

Poppy was willing to do anything to get away from her husband — even turn Tom into a killer.

BY ELLIOT WEST

TAG had been standing near the pick-up truck when the double-barrel shotgun exploded. He'd screamed once, and then the blast of shot had caught him squarely in the chest and slammed him back against the truck. Now he lay face down in the loose dirt, twitching a little, like a snake pinned beneath a heavy rock. Finally the twitching stopped and he lay limp and still.

I looked away from Tag and stared at Jake Cafree. The muzzle of Jake's shotgun was still smoking. He held the gun loosely now, but still pointed at the man he had killed.

Jake's fat, unshaven face was sweating and his thick red lips were pursed, as if he were going to whistle. A sudden, colorless blob of saliva whipped from the opening and to the ground. Then he looked at me and his eyes were hard and small. The shotgun swung carelessly in my direction and the sun painted two thin lines of garish tinsel along the barrels. It was like the glitter in Jake's eyes.

"You don't want to get gallant, do you?" he said thickly.

My voice sounded flat in my ears. "I don't want to get gallant," I said.

It was like paying court, saying it that way, or getting on your knees and waiting for favor. His mouth opened across broken and yellowed teeth. Even with a quart of whiskey at the bottom of his bloated belly, he knew there was no arguing with fear.

"Maybe you'd like to pick some cotton without it being yours, too," he said.

I didn't say anything.

"Maybe you don't allow as how I can shoot a man stealing what's mine," he said. He swung the gun in the cradle of his arms like they do blackboard pointers in a classroom. The muzzle led my eyes to the man on the ground. "Maybe you got fancy ideas yourself." He was beginning to get a little unsteady on his feet.

I said, "Maybe I've got one good one about walking away from here."

"Go ahead!" he shouted. "Cotton grew before you came and it ain't going to stop after you go."

"That's good," I said. "Then you won't feel too bad about me picking up my time."

His eyes shut, then opened, and I was thinking about the one filled chamber in that shotgun. I could smell the stench of the whiskey.

He was swaying and one foot reached out and stamped the ground in front of him, and I think it kept him from falling. His beet-shaped body was piled heavy on those legs; he looked spindly and under strain.

He coughed and the sound was like a bark.

"Get out," he said, spitting again. "Pick up your feet and point your damn self off my land."

"What about my time?"

"I might cut it short with a spray of shot," he said.

"I threw those tenants out like you told me to," I said.

"You wanted to go, didn't you?" he said. "Well, you better then because you ain't going to amount up to much if you stay." His eyes were small beads clouded in alcohol and avarice.

I left him standing there. He was still rocking on his feet, like the wind was carrying him. His murder was legal and the law was with him. I didn't think he would fall. Not right then.

I had a pressed suit and a couple of white shirts, and I went in the house and packed them into a suitcase. When I was leaving a few minutes later, I caught sight of her.

She was getting out of the station wagon she had just driven into the front yard. I was coming around the side of the sprawling house, from the kitchen door, and she saw me. We were at shouting distance but she didn't say anything. I guess she was afraid to.

I slowed my step until she was up the front porch and in the door, and then I headed for the main road. The sun was dropping in the afternoon sky. The land was flat and empty, and the big house grew small as I moved away from it. It would soon be dark.

I got a lift to town on a truck of fertilizer.

The night was a whore with

a scarlet-tinged mouth. It leaned against lamp posts. It moved through the hot streets, unbridled, and undulating like an uncorseted woman. It hung heavy in the bars and dance halls. It wasn't subtle. It was making offers but no one was taking. At least I wasn't. I had no use for it. All I had use for was throwing cards at a hat in my room at the best, worst and only hotel in town.

The phone rang. I picked up the receiver and mumbled an uncordial, "Yeah?"

"It's me. Poppy. I'm downstairs. Can I come up?"

A few seconds went by. "All right," I said finally. "Come on up."

It seemed like the receiver was hardly back in its cradle when a set of slim knuckles punched out a hurry call on the door. I let her in, but I didn't shout hooray. Or even hello.

"You've got to take me with you," she said.

"You're crazy, kid," I said.

"I wouldn't slow you down, Tom. Honest to God I wouldn't."

"I said no," I told her. "If you can't hear it, watch my lips and read it."

I sat down on the bed and she sidesaddled a spot right next to me, letting her skirt ride up to about six inches above the kneecap. It looked good, just as good as the rest of her.

"You like to hear me say it, don't you?" she said softly. "You know I can't stay here now, with you going."

"You've got a husband," I said. "Remember?"

"Him! With the fat that hangs on him, and the way he sweats and looks and talks . . . I hate him!"

"Count the ways you hate him someplace else," I said.

"You hate him, too," she said. "But you're scared."

Poppy was this country. I wanted to be rid of this country. "That could be," I told her. "Now you better get out of here."

She took a deep breath. Her breasts pushed out, high and firm and pointed. The way she filled up space was pure torture. Her body was something to see before you died. Her long brown hair flipped across one shoulder as she leaned forward suddenly.

"Tom . . ." she began.

"I've got a bus to catch," I told her.

"There's another bus in the morning."

"Always take the first one, or you might miss them all."

For a moment I thought she was going to hit me. "What bus am *I* waiting for, huh? Tell me that, if you're so damn smart."

"I just know you're here," I said. "I don't know about after that."

"My father was a dirt farmer," she said. "*That's* why I'm here. That's why I'm married to Jake." She made his name sound like all the four-letter words in the world. "I had lint in my hair and I couldn't of scraped the dirt off me with a razor, it was that thick, when he got me, but he didn't care."

"Why tell me this?" I said, impatient.

"I was glad to go with him."

"Okay, then."

She swallowed hard. "You figure it's okay for me whatever it is, don't you?" she said. "You figure I'm good for nothing but sleeping with."

I started to stand up and she went on, her voice swift and sultry hot. "I'm not good enough, and all of a sudden you're in a big hurry to get out."

I was on my feet. "I'm tired of looking at cotton and watching that no one steals it." And I heard my words with fright, realizing that I had taken on the tenor of their speech down here too, as well as other things.

"Funny," she said, mean and almost shrill, "how a fat wheezing pig can scare a man that stands on two feet."

"How many pigs do you know that can drink a quart of bonded whiskey in one sitting?"

"And carry a whip?"

"I wouldn't know about the whip," I said.

"All right," she said. "Go ahead and run. Don't even go back to pick up your time. You might have to look at him."

"I might have to look at you."

"You bastard," she said. "You yellow bastard."

I collected the cards, put on my hat and picked up my suitcase. She followed me out to the hall and down to the street.

The color of the night was uneven, like the sidewalk outside the hotel, and the redness had faded from a sky punched with holes of starlight.

"Where are you going?" she said tensely. The southern night danced in her eyes.

I started walking. I glanced back at her once. The last thing I saw were her eyes, this time with the complete darkness of stifled rage.

I walked along the dimly lit and almost deserted street to the pharmacy, now closed, at the end of a short row of squalid buildings. The bus would stop in front of the pharmacy in a few minutes and I would get on it and head north, away from Poppy and Jake and their blood-drenched farms, and a foreman named Tag who would no longer be around.

It takes a long time to make the gaunt lines in a man's face look the way they do. The way peculiar to this land. Like the face of the tall, bent man standing near me in the dark. With him it had taken somewhere around forty years of dying, not living, in this land and growing someone else's cotton till he could taste it. And it made the wretched, knob-like appearance of shadeless eyes peering at me with mute concentration.

He was standing in the dust of the road, a few feet away, and a step below where I was on the board sidewalk in front of the pharmacy. He was wearing sleazy, faded overalls and some kind of shapeless felt hat whose brim was pulled down low over a leathery face streaked with time and harsh sunlight.

I knew him. I had moved him and his wife and three children from their house a day before. His name was Dodd.

I was lighting a cigarette when he came up to me. I watched the flame, not him, and I said, "What are you staring at?"

He was immobile. "Maybe a man," he said. "Maybe not."

I stood looking at him for a moment and he looked right back. I couldn't tell where the dust ended and he began, or even if anything was real in the queer lights being thrown from the sky. I could not stare him down.

"Where do we live now, my family and me?" he said.

"Why ask me? I don't own the farms. I don't even work for them now."

It was as if I hadn't spoken. "I could buy into a tract in Kansas."

"Grab it," I said.

"It takes a thousand dollars," he said. "And mister, I ain't got a thousand dollars."

I moistened my lips. "Maybe you'd like to stand up here on the walk a while and I'll stand down there . . . change places. Okay?"

He didn't say it right away, but when he did he said it good. It was the first time his voice had had any quality or tone.

"Change places with you, mister?" he said. "I wouldn't change places with you even if all I could do was die instead."

The bus came by a few minutes after he was gone. A couple of minutes later, it left. I watched it go. Then I turned and walked back to the hotel.

Early the next day I thumbed a ride out to Jake Cafree's house. I hadn't slept very much, and with eyes still clogged in sleep I found myself on the porch in front of the door. I knocked.

When the door opened I saw that the night had been kind to Poppy. Her face was clear, and her eyes were dark and surprised. I pushed past her and into the house. I heard the door slam behind me and felt her fingers catch me at the elbow and hang themselves there.

"I thought you wouldn't have guts enough," she said.

"Where's Jake?" I said.

Her eyes were almost cat-like. "Off somewhere," she said. She came close and her hands went up to my shoulders.

"Get off," I said curtly.

Her lips were moist and they were parted just enough to bare her teeth. She was pulling my face down to hers. "Kiss me . . ." she breathed.

I untied her wrists from around my neck. "Kiss yourself," I told her. "I came for my pay. There's a tract of land in Kansas that interests me and I'll need my pay to buy into it."

"You get what's coming to you," she said. "And then we can get away. Just you and me."

"Not we . . . just me."

Her face was on fire. It was spreading and I was right in its path. Every muscle it takes to make rage in a face and body went to work in hers. She started to say something but never finished it. Footsteps, heavy and familiar, hit the front porch.

My hand was inside my jacket, touching along my pants belt, and I saw her face grow still and hard. Her breasts rose and fell in very distinct outlines against the paper-thin dress she was wearing. I closed my fingers around the .45 and waited.

The first thing I saw was Jake Cafree's face. I aimed the gun at his broken teeth.

"Close the door," I said.

He got nine-tenths sober and the shotgun in his right hand started to lift slowly from the floor.

"Don't get cute," I said. "You wouldn't look any better with a hole in the back of your neck."

His face was still as dirty as always, and just as fat and mean. His shirt was popping out at the puff around his belt-line like it didn't want to be next to him. I watched his eyes filling with blue lights of hate. I was close to shaking with the same thing.

He pushed the door shut and said nothing. He shot a quick look at her, and I did, too. It was poker, and her face hadn't picked sides yet.

"Walk into the front room," I told him.

He didn't move right away, and all I could hear was his breathing. I dropped the level of the gun to where I could have shot his navel out.

Suddenly the whiskey voice jumped from his stomach. "I don't scare easy," he growled. "And I ain't surprised."

"I'm not interested," I said. "Eight hundred dollars . . . that's all that interests me. Get it."

"Go to hell," he said. He was standing about ten feet from me, the shotgun dangling. Poppy was standing in silence near the door. I didn't let her out of my sight.

"You was ready to upchuck your guts yesterday, it made you so sick to be here," he said. "You didn't give a damn about the money then. You just wanted to go in one piece."

"I threw a man and his family out into starvation. That's worth my back pay if nothing better."

"Figure to be at peace with your soul that way?" he asked harshly.

"I'd hate to think I was being haunted free of charge," I said. I snapped my gun wrist toward the small battered desk near the window. "Hurry up, Cafree. I keep seeing Tag, and he's making me nervous."

Poppy took two slow steps toward her husband. But she wasn't looking at him. She was looking at me. "Don't let him bluff you, Jake," she said. "He ain't got guts enough to pull the trigger."

I said, "The way I learned it, you squeeze a trigger, not pull it."

She was almost yelling, glaring at me. "Squeeze or pull, you ain't got guts enough!"

"Shut up," Jake rasped. A trickle of saliva had slipped from inside to the corner of his mouth.

"He's bluffing, Jake!" she screamed. "Bluff! Bluff! Bluff!" Her whole body trembled. "Kill him!" She was staring straight into my eyes, and now I knew what she was up to. She was trying to goad Jake into trying to use the shotgun, but not because she wanted me killed. It was Jake she wanted killed, and she knew that he'd never be able to get those shotgun barrels up before I stopped him with the .45.

Jake's loose lips twisted with a curse. "I want a drink," he said.

"The money, first," I said. "Get it."

"Don't let him bluff you, honey," Poppy said. "He wouldn't shoot a tin can."

Jake's eyes grew absent and I knew that he was hearing her voice somewhere amidst the pitch and roll of alcohol in his head.

"He won't do nothing, honey," she said. "Him and his big talk and his weak stomach. Tell him you ain't scared to take that gun."

He heard her. He looked at me.

"His hand is shaking right now," she said.

He moved toward me, pushed forward by the flood of Poppy's words. He came so close to me his belly almost touched the .45.

The gun came out of my hand like it was a baby's rattle. All he did was take it.

She looked as though a stake had been driven through her. Her eyes were heavy with pain.

Well, sometimes things happen that way and people are put together like me. All you know is the inside of your own little vacuum, and everything has the futility of trying to put water back in a faucet once it's out. What it looks like on the outside doesn't bother you much. It didn't bother me.

Jake's hand trembled slightly as he laid the .45 on the desk behind him. He poured whiskey, from a pocket flask to a drinking glass on the desk. No one was talking.

Then he said, "Thought you was so goddam far above worrying about money." He was almost docile.

I had moved to the door and her body, tensed like an animal's, was blocking it.

"Leaving for someplace?" he said.

"I think so."

He was drinking with his head tossed back so far that I thought for a moment he'd lose his balance. I watched him and knew he hadn't taken my gun. I had given it to him.

"Go ahead," he said. "The air's getting jazzed up in here."

I started to move but she stood in front of me. "You ain't letting him leave?" she shouted. "You ain't letting him walk away, just like that?"

"Shut up," Jake said, drinking some more.

I started to push her aside, but she was strong and she stood her ground. "You ain't letting him walk away?" she said again. "After what he done?"

"He ain't done nothing," Jake growled. "He's just got too much milk in his water. If he didn't, he would of plugged me."

"You don't know what he done," she said. "You don't know what he said and tried to do to me."

He turned and faced where we stood like two pitchfork prongs. His face was angry, and it was focused on me. It was the same mean face that had watched Tag die.

"He asked me to run off with him," Poppy said. "He told me how he couldn't look at my body without wanting it for himself. He wanted me to leave you. But I wouldn't, honey . . ."

Jake lunged forward a few steps.

"He tried to put his hands all over me," Poppy said. "All over me!"

"You're lying," I said. "You're lying yourself into a furnace job, sure as death."

But Jake Cafree had nothing better to believe in. "So it was you," he rasped. "It was you and not Tag."

I saw it now. He hadn't killed Tag just for stealing cotton. There'd been a much better reason.

I knocked Poppy out of my path and she slammed against the door frame. Then I was running through the front door and I could hear Jake screaming all the curse words I'd ever heard, and moving drunkenly after me. I heard shrill sounds spring from Poppy's throat as my feet hit the hard clay of the path leading from the front porch to the gate.

He was drunk and I was a moving target. But there was a blast from the shotgun just as I was scrambling through the gate, and it was good enough. I felt myself torn open somewhere around the shoulder. I fell flat, face down. I could taste the dirt and my face was smeared with it.

There was another loud noise with a dull ring to it. Not a shotgun this time, and its missile didn't come in my direction. I knew that Poppy had found the courage to shoot Jake herself, with the .45 he'd left on the desk. A hoarse scream pierced the gray haze slowly enveloping my head. There was blood. There was blackness.

When I came back to consciousness, Poppy's face was clear and distinct above me. My head was propped in the crook of her arm, and the side of my face was pressed against the pillow of her breasts. I could feel the soft, warm flesh of them where the dress stopped and she began. She was on her knees beside me and the dress fell away from her like a hammock as she bent over me.

"You won't die," she said. "I

won't let you." She tugged at my armpits. "The car's just a couple of feet. I can get you to a doctor."

She got me to the station wagon. The motor growled softly as she threw it into gear and then glided along the dirt road.

"I wanted you dead," she said. "Better than letting you leave. I'd of rather had you dead."

I didn't answer.

"It'll be all right now," she said. "It'll be just us."

"What are you?" I said. "What's inside of you?"

"A dirt farm," she said. "And a whip. Did you ever see the welts on my back, or was it too dark?"

"It was too dark," I said.

The car slowed and stopped with a jolt. She unbuttoned the top of her dress with hasty, desperate fingers and slipped it down from her shoulders. She leaned forward and twisted her torso so that her bare back was in front of my face. "Look at them, Tom," she said. "Look at them, goddam it!" There were welts, reddish-purple and ugly on the smooth white skin.

I looked away from her and out the window at the flat, sun-soaked emptiness of the land. Several seconds went by.

"Say something!" she screamed at me. "Damn your soul, *say* something!" She had twisted her head around so that I could see her eyes.

"I don't want you, Poppy," I said. "Of all the women in the world I want you the least."

She was still leaning across me. I watched her slender fingers move to the glove compartment and open it. Sunlight glinted on a flat pint whiskey bottle. Her fingers touched the bottle, almost lovingly, and then her fingers were pushing the bottle aside, probing behind it.

Suddenly her body jerked and her hand was coming out again. The sun glinted on something besides the bottle now.

There was an unsheathed hunting knife in Poppy's hand and it was blurring toward my stomach.

The land is flat and the horizon is like a diagonal line from where I watch. The sun is high in the middle of the day, searing the earth like an acetylene torch.

Poppy's voice hangs in the air now like the faint, distant ring after a gong has been struck. "Then bleed," she'd said. "Bleed white and die, goddam you, Tom." And then she'd driven away.

It is red and wet on the ground and cotton will not grow here. I lie where she rolled me from the front seat.

Something black is in the sky. It is winged and circling. Slowly.

Evidence

Reuter got Lucille to take part in an insurance fraud. And then he had her right where he wanted her.

A Johnny Liddell Story

BY FRANK KANE

HER VOICE sounded throaty and sultry over the phone.

When she opened the door in response to Johnny Liddell's knock, it was obvious that the voice belonged. She was tall. Her red hair was piled on top of her head, and a blue silk gown did its best to cover her lovely figure. Her lips were full, moist, soft, her eyes green and slightly slanted.

"You're Johnny Liddell?" The slanted eyes hop-scotched from the

broad shoulders to the face, approvingly. "Won't you come in?" She stood aside, took his hat as he walked by. "I've been expecting you."

"I got over as soon as I could, Mrs. Hart," Liddell told her.

She led the way into an expensively-furnished living room. As she walked, her hips worked smoothly against the fragile fabric of the gown. It was highly debatable whether or not she wore anything under it.

"Will you have a drink?" she asked. "*I* certainly can use one."

Liddell nodded, dropped down on the couch, watched her until she disappeared into the kitchen. When she returned, the view from the front was equally satisfying. She set the bottle and glasses down on a small table in front of the sofa, sat down alongside him. "I need your help very badly, Mr. Liddell," she said. "I've gotten into something over my head."

Liddell nodded. "Mind filling me in?"

The redhead caught her lower lip between her teeth, worried it. "It makes me feel like such a fool." She leaned over with devastating effect to the low neckline of her gown, spilled some liquor into each of the glasses. "It all started a little over a year ago. I was married to Ed Hart at the time."

Liddell picked up his glass, swirled the liquor around the sides. "You're not now?"

The redhead pursed her lips, shook her head. "We were divorced almost six weeks ago." She held up her glass. "Will you drink with me to my freedom?"

Liddell grinned, clicked his glass against hers. "Then there's really no need to keep calling you Mrs. Hart, since you aren't."

"I'm Lucille." She sipped at her drink, studied him over the rim. "You know, I feel better about telling you this story already. I have the feeling you'll understand."

"Try me."

The girl tossed off the rest of her drink, set her glass down. "I guess you'd really have to know Ed Hart to understand it. He was dead set against gambling or drinking. Pretty strait-laced." She shrugged, leaned over, added some more liquor to her glass. "I put up with it because —" she looked up at Liddell, the soft lips smiling. "I put up with it because he was what I'd been gunning for since the day I left Ohio. A millionaire."

Liddell showed no signs of being shocked.

"But just the same, I liked to take a little fling at the tracks or at a card game." She shrugged. "I didn't figure there was any harm in it."

"But he would have."

"He would have been furious. So I just didn't tell him."

Liddell nodded, picked two cigarettes out of the humidor on the table, lighted them, passed one to the girl. "And you lost more than you intended to."

The redhead nodded. "I guess I

don't have a copyright on this story." She took a deep drag on the cigarette. "I went for about five thousand more than I intended. I had enough IOUs floating around to paper a good-sized room. And then they lowered the boom."

"Who had your paper?"

The redhead lifted the cigarette from between her lips, studied the carmined end with distaste. "A nasty little chiseler named Carl Reuter. Know him?"

"Just what I read about him in the gossip columns. And that's not very pretty."

"He's even crummier than that." She took a swallow from her glass, appeared to be washing the taste of his name from her mouth. "He married old Madeline Stewart when she didn't have all her marbles and spent most of the rest of her life going through her money. He pays his rent these days by playing cards with the right people."

Liddell nodded. "And you were his pigeon."

The redhead shrugged. "I figured it was only money and that I'd be able to square it with him as soon as Ed Hart came across with either an allowance or a settlement."

"But?"

"Carl got itchy. He said he needed the money right away and suggested that I tell Ed about it. The implication was pretty clear that if I didn't, he would." She finished her drink, leaned back against the cushion, her breasts jutting forward against her robe. "That would have spoiled everything. So then he got another idea."

Liddell fought a losing struggle to keep his eyes on her face, lost it happily. "What was that?"

"I had no money, but Ed kept me well decked out in jewelry. I guess it made him feel like a big shot. Anyway, it was insured for twenty thousand. Carl suggested we fake a robbery and collect the twenty thousand and I could pay him off with the jewels. He said he had a contact who could get rid of them for him."

Liddell groaned, freshened up both drinks. "And you went for that set-up?"

"I went for it. Me, the smart babe who knew all the answers. It looked like an easy out. Carl gets the jewels and sells them for at least what I owe him. We get the insurance money to keep my husband happy and nobody gets hurt. That's a laugh!" She put her hand on his knee, leaned over. "I was even dumb enough to send him a letter with the jewels saying that I was paying him off with them."

Liddell nodded. "And he's been bleeding you ever since."

The redhead nodded. "Mercilessly." She got up, walked to the window, stared down into the street below. "I can't take much more of it. What can I do?"

"He's got you pretty much over a barrel," Liddell said. "He's got your letter saying you gave him the jewels as payment for a loan. And you made the claim to the insurance company that they were stolen and took the money." He shook his head. "I don't suppose he'd sell the letter back?"

She turned, walked back to where he sat, the sway of her breasts tracing designs on the shiny silk of her robe. She stopped in front of him. "I've done everything to get it back. Everything that's humanly possible. I tried to make a deal — but he wasn't interested in me." She wet her lips with the tip of her tongue, her eyes half-lidded. "Would you be interested in a deal like that, Liddell?"

Liddell's eyes ran over her. "I haven't got the letter, baby."

"You might be able to get it — if it were worth your while." She raised her hand to her neck, fumbled with the zipper. With a quick motion, she unzipped the front of the gown, slid it back off her shoulders, stepped out of it.

She was breath-takingly curved. Her legs were long. Shapely calves became full rounded thighs above the knee. Her high-set hips converged into a narrow waist and a stomach as flat as an athlete's. Her breasts were full and round, their pink tips straining continually upward. She brought her hands up from her sides, released her hair to fall in a molten cascade over her shoulders.

She stood there.

Liddell reached up, caught her by the hand, pulled her down to him. She reached up, buried her fingers in his hair, pulled his mouth down to hers. Her lips were soft, eager.

After a moment, he pulled back, breathed hard. "You make it tough for a guy to refuse, baby," he told her.

She smiled up at him. "I intended to." She caught his tie, loosened it, unbuttoned his collar.

She pulled his face down again. As his mouth found hers, she shuddered uncontrollably. Her nails dug into his shoulders, and he could feel her sharp little teeth gnawing at his lip. He kissed her neck, her ear . . .

"A guy'd being willing to kill somebody for a deal like you," he said.

"I'm hoping you will," she told him.

Carl Reuter was listed in the telephone book as living in the Settler Arms, an expensive pile of rocks and plate glass overlooking Riverside Drive. Johhny Liddell plowed through the deep-pile carpeting to the desk, asked the tired-looking man in the morning coat for Reuter's apartment number.

"Is Mr. Reuter expecting you?" the man asked.

Liddell considered, shook his head. "Tell him I'm representing a Mrs. Hart," he suggested. "It's in reference to the sale of some property."

The tired-looking man nodded, disappeared into a small office, reappeared after a few seconds. "It's the Penthouse." He nodded in the direction of a bank of elevators. "The end cage."

Liddell walked to the elevator, rode to the Penthouse. He rapped on the door, waited. After a moment the door was opened, and a man stood in the doorway. Liddell couldn't make out the man's features, but from the bulging shoulders and complete absence of neck, it didn't strain his deductive powers to place him as a professional bodyguard.

"You the guy the desk phoned up about?" His voice was heavy, rough.

"Yeah. Is Reuter in?"

The bodyguard nodded him through a darkened vestibule into what appeared to be a library. In the light the man turned out to have bulging eyebrows and a misshapen nose in keeping with the bulging shoulders. There was a dark shadow of a beard on his jowls. His small eyes were suspicious as he looked Liddell over.

"You heeled?" he asked.

Liddell shook his head. "This is a social call." He offered no resistance when the butler fanned him, satisfied himself Liddell was unarmed. "Mr. Reuter's in the den." He led the way down a corridor with a surprisingly light foot for a man of his weight. At the far end, a door led into a comfortably furnished den.

Carl Reuter sat behind a highly-polished desk. He didn't raise his eyes from the five-inch switch knife with which he was manicuring his nails. He was thin and dapper. His thick hair was shiny, and he affected a three-quarter part designed to give his widow's peak its best play. His face was almost perfectly oval. The only thing that spoiled his good looks was his thin lips.

"What do you want, Liddell?"

"You've got something to sell. I want to buy."

Reuter raised his eyes from his nails, tested the blade of the knife against his thumb, dropped his eyes again. "You must have me mixed up with somebody else. I have nothing to sell. Who sent you here?"

"Let's stop playing coy with each other, Reuter. You have some evidence. It's paid for itself a dozen times over already, but I'm ready to buy it again. This time permanently."

"Sit down, Liddell," the little man said. When Liddell showed no sign of accepting the invitation, the butler grabbed him by the arm, shoved him into a chair. "That's better." Reuter got up from behind the desk, walked to where Liddell sat, pointed with the knife so that its tip was less than an inch from Liddell's throat. "I've heard all about what a tough guy you are. But I'm not impressed. Be smart and quit while you're still ahead."

"You're scaring me to death," Liddell said. "It's like I told your boy. This is just a social call. If I come back, it'll be for business."

The knife at his throat didn't waver. Finally, Reuter shrugged. "What good would that do Lucille?" he said. "If anything happens to me, plenty of evidence against her goes to the district attorney." He pasted a leering smile on his lips. "Wouldn't it be a shame to lock that chassis in a cage for ten or fifteen years?" He jabbed suddenly with the knife, nicked the skin on Liddell's neck. "It would be very foolish of you to show your face around here again. Ever."

Liddell touched his finger where the knife had broken his skin, examined the drop of blood on his finger. "I have an idea that we'll continue this discussion under more favorable conditions, pal." Suddenly, he lashed out with his heel, caught the little man in the shin.

Reuter howled, dropped his knife, clasped his shin in both hands.

The butler swore under his breath, grabbed Liddell by the lapels, dragged him to his feet. The private detective broke the hold with an upward and outward fling of his arms, smashed his toe into the big man's instep. The butler roared with pain, dropped his guard. Liddell sank his left into the other man's middle, chopped down against the side of his jaw with a right. The butler hit the floor without a sound, lay there.

Reuter leaned against the desk, glared at Liddell. "I'll get you for this, Liddell," he said. "Nobody pushes me around. And you're crazy if you think this does that babe of yours any good. I'll take care of her. You can tell her that."

Liddell looked around the den, debated the advisability of trying to find the little man's hiding place, decided against it.

"I'm giving you until midnight to get up what I came for," he told Reuter. "If you don't come up with it, I'm going to see you again. Then you'll tell me."

The little man started to sneer, but it froze on his lips as Liddell walked over to him, caught him by the front of his jacket, lifted him to his toes. A faint line of perspiration glistened suddenly at the little man's hair line. "Don't think you won't talk, Reuter. You'd be surprised how persuasive I can get." He shoved the little man backwards. "By midnight. In my office. With the material."

The man on the floor started to moan his way back to consciousness. Liddell walked over to where he lay, caught him by the collar, lifted him to a chair. "And I wouldn't figure on this guy doing you much good." He turned his back, walked to the door and punched the elevator button.

The redhead was waiting in a car on the block north of the Settler Arms. Liddell slid into the front seat next to her.

"How'd it go?" she asked.

Liddell shrugged. "He's a hard little cookie, but I think I threw a scare into him." He touched his finger to the nick on his neck, showed the faint smear of blood to the girl. "He sure plays rough with that sticker of his."

The redhead's eyes widened.

Liddell grinned crookedly. "But you ought to see the other guy." He half-swung in his seat, watched the entrance to the Settler Arms, from the rear window. "We'd better start keeping an eye open. If my guess is right, he'll be coming out any time now."

Lucille shook her head. "I don't think so, Liddell. Why should he? Isn't he safer up there with that big gorilla of his keeping an eye on him?"

Liddell grunted. "The last time I saw that gorilla of his he wasn't capable of keeping an eye on anything. No. If my guess is right, Reuter will try to hole up until he can put the heat on you to call me off, or until he can have someone take care of me. My guess is that Reuter isn't much of a guy for standing toe-to-toe and slugging."

The girl lit a cigarette nervously, took a deep drag. "But even if he does run, what good will that do us?" She exhaled the smoke. "Maybe he's right. Maybe I have complicated this by —"

"Look, baby. Here's the idea. We throw a scare into Reuter, he runs for his hole. Does he leave his most valuable possessions behind him?"

The redhead studied Liddell's face, the tiny frown between her eyes washed away. "You mean you think he'll take them with him?"

Liddell shrugged. "Why not? Wouldn't you?" He took the cigarette from between her lips, took a deep drag on it.

Lucille caught her full lower lip between her teeth, considered. "It makes sense at that. Then when we find out where he's hiding, you can go in and take it away from him?"

Liddell nodded. "You catch on fast."

The redhead was on her fourth cigarette when Carl Reuter walked out of the Settler Arms. He stood in front of the building, looked up and down the street. After a moment, the bulky form of his bodyguard joined him on the sidewalk. A bellhop brought out five large suitcases, piled them at the curb.

At the sight of the suitcases, the redhead said, "If it's only in that stuff, Johnny. If it's only there!"

Liddell nodded, motioned for her to sink down into the seat as a cab pulled up at the hotel and Reuter and the big man climbed in. After a moment the cab whizzed by the parked car, headed uptown.

Johnny Liddell waited until the cab was a block ahead, eased his car away from the curb, followed it.

The cab headed for 110th Street, bore right, stopped in the middle of the block between Park and Madison. Liddell drove slowly past, marked the number in his mind. Reuter and the big man were too busy taking care of the baggage to pay any attention to his car.

Liddell drove to the corner of Madison, pulled the car to the curb. "Take the car back to your place," he told the redhead. "I'll stake out here and wait until one or the other leave. Then maybe we can check up on my hunch." He took his shoulder harness and a .45 from the glove compartment, took off his jacket, slid into it, covered it with the jacket.

Lucille wet her lips nervously with her tongue. "Do you really think he'll have it with him, Johnny?" She leaned against him. "If he has, and you get it back, I'll never be able to tell you how much it means to me."

Liddell grinned. "You made a pretty good start this morning, baby."

After the car had melted into the downtown traffic on Madison, Liddell crossed 110th to a small store, bought a pack of cigarettes. He stood in the front of the store, watched the doorway across the street through its grimy window. After about an hour, he went out, leaned against the far side of the building where he'd be invisible to anyone in one of the windows.

The early heat of the day started to cool off as the shadows got longer. Liddell was debating the advisability of waiting until evening and then, if necessary, facing both men when the door opened. The bodyguard stepped out, stood on the stoop, looked in both directions. He pulled a cigarette from his pocket, lit it, stood smoking for a moment. Then, he walked down the steps, blended into the stream of whites, browns, yellows and blacks that ebb and flow the length of 110th Street twenty-four hours a day.

Liddell waited until the big man had reached the corner of Park, and then he crossed the street. He walked up the short stoop of the house where Reuter had gone earlier.

He entered the foul-smelling vestibule, looked around. There were no mailboxes, merely a few scribbled sex suggestions in pencil and chalk. Several were illustrated, but seemed impractical.

Liddell pushed through the inner door to the hallway. Here an odor, compounded of equal parts of old cooking, perspiration and inadequate toilet facilities was almost gagging. As he walked in, an old man in a dirty undershirt came up from the cellar stairs at the back of the hall. The old man stared at Liddell suspiciously through a pair of small metal-rimmed glasses. He took a short-stemmed pipe from between toothless gums, spat on the floor. His eyes never left Liddell.

"I'm looking for the new tenant. The one that moved in today," Liddell said. "I forgot what apartment he told me."

The old man continued to stare, spat again. He watched while Liddell reached into his pocket, brought out a bill, folded it lengthwise. He wiped the palm of his hand along the seam of his pants, reached out. "Two

C." His voice was beery, coarse. "There'll be no trouble, mister?"

Liddell grinned, shook his head. "No trouble. He's an old pal." He walked to the uncarpeted, grimy stairs, started up.

Two C was the second door off the stair well. Liddell listened outside for a moment, tried the knob. The door was locked. He could hear the whisper of motion from the other side.

"That you, Benny?" A muffled voice came through the door.

"Yeah." Liddell made his voice gruff, raspy.

There was the sound of a chain being removed, a key turned in the lock. The door opened a crack, and before Reuter could get set, Liddell put his shoulder against it, pushed it open.

The little man swore under his breath. There was a flash of steel, and the tip of his knife jabbed Liddell just above the belt line.

"How'd you get here?" he asked.

"I just followed the smell. You leave a stink a foot wide."

"You sure want it bad, sucker," Reuter said. His tongue wet his purple-red lips, retreated back into his mouth. The sleepy eyes looked malevolent, lethal, half-veiled by discolored lids. He looked beyond Liddell into the hall, satisfied himself that the private detective was alone, motioned him into the room. He shoved the door closed with his foot, locked it with his hand behind him. "Nice of you to save us the trouble of going out to look for you. Now I won't have to stay in this rathole any longer than it takes to get rid of you."

Liddell looked around the squalidly-furnished room. "Not quite as fancy as the Settler Arms is it, Reuter? I guess, though, you figured it's better to live in a rathole than to stop living completely."

Reuter smoothed the hair back over his ears, using his fingers as a comb. "Speak for yourself, shamus. I expect to go on living. Too bad you can't say the same, huh?" He jabbed the point of the knife into Liddell's back. "Get those hands up over your head where I can watch them."

Liddell laced his fingers at the back of his neck, permitted Reuter to reach around him to relieve him of the gun he'd taken from the car. The man with the knife made the mistake of getting too close while doing it. Liddell pivoted at the waist, the point of his elbow catching the shorter man in the temple. Reuter staggered, tried to slash out with the knife.

Liddell swung around, brought up his knee viciously, simultaneously chopped at the side of Reuter's neck with the side of his hand. Reuter uttered a choked grunt, dropped the knife. He stood swaying for a brief instant, then his knees folded under him. He went to his knees, fell over forward face first, slid out full length, didn't move.

Liddell replaced his .45 in its holster, picked up the knife that had fallen from Reuter's fingers, tossed it on the table. He turned the unconscious man over, went through his pockets. There was almost a hundred dollars in bills, a handful of silver, an alligator wallet. There were no baggage checks or checkroom receipts of any kind.

Liddell took Reuter's key chain, turned his attention to the bags he'd brought with him. After fifteen minutes, he knew that what he was looking for wasn't in any of the valises nor was it on the man's person. He picked up Reuter's knife, slit the sides of the bags, dumped the contents on the floor. As a last resort, he stripped the bedding from the bed. The thing he was looking for was under the mattress.

It was a thick brief case. He dug into it, satisfied himself that it contained photostats of IOUs, letters from women telling Reuter that they were turning over their jewels to satisfy gambling debts, clippings from newspapers detailing jewel robberies. He dumped the papers back into the brief case.

Reuter was moaning his way back to consciousness. Liddell reached over, dragged him to a chair. Carl Reuter was no longer dapper. The thin purple lips were now blue, the eyes watery and the carefully combed hair hung down over his face. He was sick. His head rolled uncontrollably from side to side. He seemed to lack the power to lift it.

"Listen hard, Reuter," Liddell told him. "You're finished. I'm destroying these letters and the IOUs. Then I'm tipping the cops off to the racket you've been pulling. If you're smart, you won't be here when they get here."

There was a light tap on the door. Liddell walked over, put his lips close to the door. "That you, Benny?" he whispered.

The voice on the other side was urgent. "Yeah, Reuter. Let me in."

Liddell carefully unlocked the door, pulled it open. The bodyguard's eyes popped when he recognized the detective. He started to raise his hands, but his reflexes were too slow. Liddell hit him in the stomach with a straight left, slammed a right to his jaw. The big man reeled backwards. Liddell hit him again with a straight right, driving him still further back. The low banister caught his back, gave way with a screech and the big man disappeared into the black well of the stairway.

Heads popped out from doorways all along the hall, were withdrawn as though they were on strings. Liddell stood at the head of the stairs, looked down at the tangle of arms and legs that were the big man.

The old man in the dirty undershirt looked up the stairs, removed the pipe from between his gums, shook his head. "You said there wouldn't be no trouble, mister," he reproved. Liddell shrugged sadly, turned to re-enter the room.

As he did, a shadow melted out of the darker shadows in the hall. Liddell did a double-take, stared at the girl with an open mouth. "I thought you were going back to your place."

"I couldn't let you go up against those two alone, Johnny," the redhead told him. "I didn't realize how good you really were." She walked into the room, sneered at Reuter. "*He* just talked tough, I guess." Her eyes roved around the room, came to rest on the brief case. She ran to it. "You got it!"

"You'd better be getting out of here, baby," Liddell advised. "The cops are going to show up any time now to find out what the fight's all about. Leave that here. I'll take care of destroying the stuff on you."

The redhead shook her head. "I'd better take it with me."

"Don't argue," Liddell said. "There's stuff in there about other people —"

A small gun had appeared in the girl's hand. "I know all about what's in here. There's a goldmine in here and whoever owns it is in the saddle. I don't intend to stand up and give anybody my seat."

Liddell's eyes narrowed. "What is this?"

"I thought maybe you'd guessed by now, Liddell. Reuter wasn't blackmailing me. I was his partner in the racket. I set the biddies up for him, saw to it they lost. He thought he could muscle me out of my share of the cut."

Liddell growled under his breath, started toward the girl.

A strained look appeared between her eyes, and her finger whitened on the trigger. "Don't make the mistake of thinking I won't shoot. Reuter had the Indian sign on me because he had the evidence that I was part of the racket here. Now, nobody can prove it."

Liddell kept walking toward her. The little gun in her hand belched. Liddell felt the slug pull at his sleeve.

"That's just to show you I'll shoot," she told him. The gun in her hand was steady, swung to cover his midsection. "You'll get the next one in the belly."

Liddell looked into the muzzle of the little gun, swore.

"You can't take two of us, baby," a voice from behind growled.

Liddell whirled in time to see Carl Reuter leaning against the table, his knife between his thumb and forefinger. The redhead's eyes moved from Liddell to the little man. She swung her gun, squeezed the trigger frantically. The first slug hit him at almost the instant his knife left his fingers. He fell back over the table, dumped it to the floor with him.

Liddell turned. The redhead stood facing him. The handle of the knife protruded from her abdomen like some obscene horn. She dropped the gun, wrapped both hands around the handle of the knife, tried to tug it free. She swayed for a moment, toppled to the ground.

She was dead by the time Liddell turned her over.

Portrait of a Killer

No. 2—Charles Henry Schwartz

BY DAN SONTUP

He never liked to use his own name — especially when he was making a play for some woman — so he used a different name for almost every woman he had.

At home, in California, he was plain Charles Henry Schwartz — a chemist, a married man with a wife and three young sons. But, away from home, he was a dapper, smooth-talking little Romeo. He had small, dainty hands and feet, polished manners, and the ability to tell beautiful lies with a straight face.

He got lots of women with these tactics, but it all finally caught up with him. When one of his conquests found out that she'd been taken for a ride, she called for her lawyer and started legal proceedings.

That was when Schwartz decided to vanish — and he arranged a murder to cover up his disappearance.

He decided to make use of the gimmick of having a corpse take his place, so that once he was assumed dead, he could go on as before without any worries at all. He knew of other men who had tried this and failed, but, he told himself, Charles Henry Schwartz was smarter. He worked long and hard on his scheme and finally had it perfected.

Most of the plan was already set up for him. He had already arranged a very complicated set of life insurance policies that would take care of his wife and family after his death. (Whether or not he planned to try and cash in on this later, no one knows.) Next, he made use of a factory which he had purchased, so he told everyone, for the purpose of manufacturing artificial silk. He had what he called a laboratory there, and no one was allowed to enter but himself. As far as anyone knew, Schwartz was working out secret formulae there — and that suited his purpose very well.

The first step in his plan was to claim that some foreign chemists were after his secret of making artificial silk, and that this was the real reason for the lawsuit the woman had brought. The second step was to circulate another rumor. This one was that he worked with highly explosive materials, and that he was in danger of being blown sky-high at any time. He even wrote letters to his wife and his lawyer, to be opened only in the event of his death.

Schwartz had now taken care of the preliminaries. He had planted the idea that he might be killed. He let the idea grow and develop and then he put the final stage of his plan into operation.

He hunted around until he found a man, a stranger in town, who fitted his own description pretty closely. Somehow, he talked the man into going to the secret laboratory with him, making sure that no one saw them enter. Once inside, he slugged the stranger on the back of the head, killing him outright. Then he dragged the body into a closet and left it there until nighttime.

When it was finally dark enough, Schwartz told the night watchman that he'd be working late, and that the watchman could take a nap. Once he was alone, Schwartz dragged the body out of the closet and placed it on the floor in the lab. He then proceeded to knock out some of the corpse's teeth, making sure that the teeth he removed corresponded to his own missing teeth. After that, he swabbed acid on the fingertips until all fingerprints had been completely mutilated; and then he punctured both eyeballs of the corpse so that the color of the eyes could not be determined. Finally, he placed his own watch on the body.

He sprinkled benzol over the body and along the floor, struck a match, tossed it — and took off.

He went to an apartment in a nearby city, having already rented the apartment under one of his many aliases, and holed up there and waited for the news of his death.

Sure enough, the papers carried the news the next day, and Schwartz thought he was safe. But he wasn't.

For one thing, the night watchman had awakened just in time to see the fire start. He called the fire department, and they put out the fire in pretty short order. That was Schwartz's first mistake — not sending the night watchman on an errand in order to be absolutely sure that he wouldn't be around.

The other mistakes were easily uncovered by the police. The corpse had been burned to a crisp, indicating that far too much heat had been applied to that one spot in the lab. The scorch marks on the floor also showed that the fire had been started outside the door.

A careful autopsy disclosed the fact that the teeth had been forcibly knocked out of the skull, that the man had been a bit taller than Schwartz, and that the man had been dead before the fire started. Finally, from other clues that the fire hadn't destroyed, the police were able to identify the corpse as that of an itinerant preacher.

The hunt was on for Schwartz — However, just as the police were closing in on him, Schwartz put the barrel of a pistol against his right eye and pulled the trigger.

This corpse was not unidentified — and he had left a suicide note confessing to the crime.

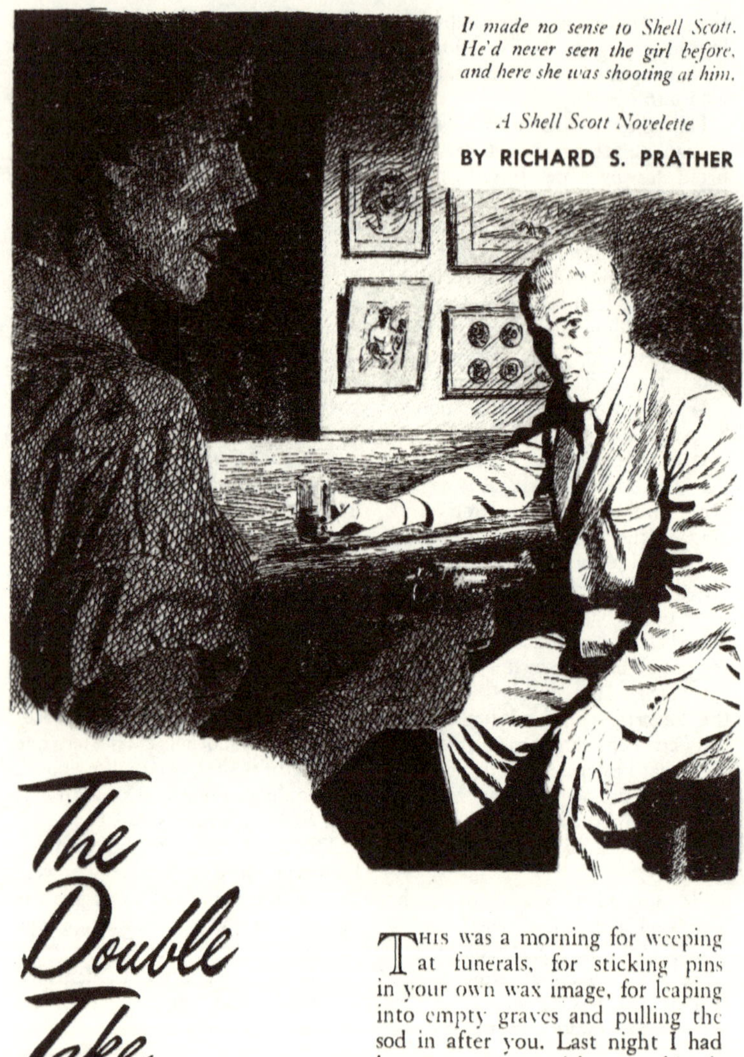

It made no sense to Shell Scott. He'd never seen the girl before, and here she was shooting at him.

A Shell Scott Novelette

BY RICHARD S. PRATHER

The Double Take

THIS was a morning for weeping at funerals, for sticking pins in your own wax image, for leaping into empty graves and pulling the sod in after you. Last night I had been at a party with some friends here in Los Angeles, and I had drunk bourbon and scotch and martinis and maybe even swamp water from highball glasses, and now my brain was a bomb that went off twice a second.

I thought thirstily of Pete's Bar downstairs on Broadway, right next door to this building, the Hamilton, where I have my detective agency, then got out of my chair, left the office and locked the door behind me. I was Shell Scott, The Bloodshot Eye, and I needed a hair of the horse that bit me.

Before I went downstairs I stopped by the PBX switchboard at the end of the hall. Cute little Hazel glanced up.

"You look terrible," she said.

"I know. I think I'm decomposing. Listen, a client just phoned me and I have to rush out to the Hollywood Roosevelt. I'll be back in an hour or so, but for the next five minutes I'll be in Pete's. Hold down the fort, huh?"

"Sure, Shell. Pete's?" She shook her head.

I tried to grin at her, whereupon she shrank back and covered her eyes, and I left. Hazel is a sweet kid, tiny, and curvy, and since mine is a one-man agency with no receptionist or secretary, the good gal tries to keep informed of my whereabouts.

I tottered down the one flight of stairs into bright June sunshine on Broadway, thinking that my client would have to wait an extra five minutes even though he'd been in a hell of a hurry. But he'd been in a hurry the last time, too, and nothing had come of it. This Frank Harrison had first called me on Monday morning, three days ago, and insisted I come right out to his hotel in Hollywood. When I got there he explained that he was having marital troubles and wanted me to tail his wife and see if I could catch her in any indiscretions. When I told him I seldom handled that kind of job, he'd said to forget it, so I had. The deal had seemed screwy; he'd not only been vague, but hadn't pressed me much to take the case. It had added up to an hour wasted, and no fee.

But this morning when I'd opened the office at nine sharp the phone had been ringing and it was Harrison again. He wanted me right away this time, too, but he had a real case for me, he said, not like last time, and it wasn't tailing his wife. He was in a sweat to get me out to the Roosevelt's bar, the Cinegrill where we were to meet, and was willing to pay me fifty bucks just to listen to his story. I still didn't know what was up, but it sounded like a big one. I hoped it was bigger than the last "job," and, anyway, it couldn't be as big as my head. I went into Pete's.

Pete knew what I wanted as soon as I perched on a stool and he got a good look at my eyeballs, so he immediately mixed the ghastly concoction he gives me for hangovers.

I was halfway through it when his phone rang.

He listened a moment, said, "I'll tell him," then turned to me. "That was Hazel," he said. "Some dame was up there looking for you. A wild woman —"

That was as far as he got. I heard somebody come inside the front door, and high heels clicked rapidly over the floor and stopped alongside me. A woman's voice, tight and angry, said, "There you are, you, you . . . you crook!" and I turned on my stool to look at the wild woman.

I had never seen her before, but that was obviously one of the most unfortunate omissions of my life, because one look at her and I forgot my hangover. She was an absolutely gorgeous little doll, about five feet two inches tall, and any half-dozen of her sixty-two delightful inches would make any man stare, and all of her at once was enough to knock a man's eyes out through the back of his head.

"Oh!" she said. "You ought to be tarred and feathered."

I kept looking. Coal black hair was fluffed around her oval face, and though she couldn't have been more than twenty-four or twenty-five years old, a thin streak of gray ran back from her forehead through that thick, glossy hair. She was dressed in light blue clam-diggers and a man's white shirt which her chest filled out better than any man's ever did, and her eyes were an incredibly light electric blue — shooting sparks at me.

She was angry. She was so hot she looked ready to melt. It seemed, for some strange reason, she was angry with me. This lovely was not one I wanted angry with me; I wanted her happy, and patting my cheek, or perhaps even chewing on my ear.

She looked at the light blond, almost white hair that sticks up about an inch from my scalp, then at my whitish eyebrows and slightly bent nose, looked me up and down and said, "Yes. Yes, you're Shell Scott."

"That's right. Certainly. But —"

"I want that twenty-four thousand dollars and I'm going to get it if I — if I have to *kill* you! I mean it!"

"Huh?"

"It's just money to you, you crook! But it's all he had, all my father's saved in years and years. Folsom's Market, indeed! I'll kill you, I *will!* So give me that money. I know you're in with them."

My head was in very bad shape to begin with, but now I was beginning to think maybe I had mush up there. She hadn't yet said a single word that made sense.

"Take it easy," I said. "You must have the wrong guy."

If anything, that remark made her angrier. She pressed white teeth together and made noises in her throat, then she said, "I suppose you're not Shell Scott."

"Sure I am, but I don't know what you're babbling about."

"Babbling! *Babbling!* Ho, that's the way you're going to play it, are you? Going to deny everything, pretend it never happened! I knew you would! Well . . ."

She backed away from me, fumbling with the clasp of a big handbag. I looked at her thinking that one of us was completely mad. Then she dug into her bag and pulled out a chromed pistol, probably a .22 target pistol, and pointed it at me. She was crying now, her face twisted up and tears running down her cheeks, but she still appeared to be getting angrier every second, and slowly the thought seeped into my brain: This tomato is aiming a real gun at me.

She backed away toward the rear of Pete's, but she was still too close to suit me, and close enough so I could see her eyes squeeze shut and her finger tighten on the trigger. I heard the crack of the little gun and I heard a guy who had just come in the door, let out a yelp behind me, and I heard a little tinkle of glass. And then I heard a great clattering and crashing of glass because by this time I was clear over behind the bar with Pete, banging into bottles and glasses on my way down to the floor. I heard the gun crack twice more and then high heels clattered away from me and I peeked over the bar just in time to see the gal disappearing into the Ladies' Room.

A man on my left yelled, "Janet! *Jan!*" I looked at him just as he got up off the floor, and I remembered the guy who had yelped right after that first shot. He didn't seem to be hurt, though, because he got to his feet and started after the beautiful crazy gal.

He was a husky man, about five-ten, wearing brown slacks and a T-shirt which showed off his impressive chest. Even so, it wasn't as impressive as the last chest I'd seen, and although less than a minute had elapsed since I'd first seen the gal who'd been behind it, I was already understandably curious about her. I vaulted over the bar and yelled at the man, "Hey, you! Hold it!"

He stopped and jerked his head around as I stepped up in front of him. His slightly effeminate face didn't quite go with the masculine build, but many women would probably have called him "handsome" or even "darling." A thick mass of black curly hair came down in a sharp widow's peak on his white forehead. His mouth was full, chin square and dimpled, and large black-lashed brown eyes blinked at me.

"Who the hell was that tomato?" I asked him. "And what's happening?"

"You tell me," he said. And then an odd thing happened. He hadn't yet had time to take a good look at me, but he took it now. He gawked at my white hair, my face, blinked, and his mouth dropped open. "Oh, *Christ!*" he said, and then he took off. Naturally he ran into the Ladies Rest Room. It just wouldn't have seemed right at that point if he'd gone anyplace else.

I looked over my shoulder at Pete, whose mouth was hanging completely ajar, then I went to the Ladies Room and inside. Nobody was there. A wall window was open and I looked out through it at the empty alley, then looked all around the rest room again, but it was still empty.

I went back to the bar and said, "Pete, what the hell did you put in that drink?"

He stared at me, shaking his head. Finally he said, "I never seen nothing like that in my life. Thirteen years I've run this place, but . . ." He didn't finish it.

My hand was stinging and so was a spot on my chin. Going over the bar I had broken a few bottles and cut my left hand slightly, and one of those little slugs had apparently come close enough to nick my chin. I had also soaked up a considerable amount of spilled whiskey in my clothes and I didn't smell good at all. My head hadn't been helped, either, by the activity.

Pete nodded when I told him to figure up the damage and I'd pay him later, then I went back into the Hamilton Building. It appeared Frank Harrison would have to wait. Also, the way things were going, I wanted to get the .38 Colt Special and harness out of my desk.

At the top of the stairs I walked down to the PBX again. Hazel, busy at the switchboard, didn't see me come up but when I spoke she swung around. "What's with that gal you called Pete's about?" I asked her.

"She find you? Wasn't she a beautiful little thing?"

"Yeah. And she found me."

Hazel's nose was wrinkling. "You *are* decomposing," she said. "Into bourbon. How many shots did you have?"

"Three, I think. But they all missed me."

"Missed you, ha —"

"Shots that beautiful little thing took at me, I mean. With a gun."

Hazel blinked. "You're kidding." I shook my head and she said, "Well, I — she did seem upset, a little on edge."

"She was clear the hell over the edge. What did she say?"

"She asked for you. As a matter of fact, she said, 'Where's that dirty Shell Scott?' I told her you'd gone to Pete's downstairs — " Hazel smiled sweetly — "for some medicine, and she ran away like mad. She seemed very excited."

"She was."

"And a man came rushing up here a minute or two after the girl and asked about her. I said I'd sent her to Pete's — and *he* ran off." She shook her head. "I don't know. I'm a little confused."

That I could understand. Maybe it was something in the L. A. air this morning. I thanked Hazel and walked down to the office, fishing out my keys, but when I got there I noticed the door was already cracked. I shoved it open and walked inside. For the second or third time this morning my jaw dropped open. A guy was seated behind my desk, fussing with some papers on its top, looking businesslike as all hell. He was a big guy, husky, around thirty years old, with white hair sticking up into the air about an inch.

Without looking up, he said, "Be right with you."

I walked to the desk and sank into one of the leather chairs in front of it, a chair I bought for clients to sit in. If the chair had raised up and floated me out of the window while violins played in the distance, my stunned expression would not have changed one iota. In a not very strong voice I said, "Who are you?"

"I'm Shell Scott," he said briskly, glancing up at me.

Ah, yes. That explained it. He was Shell Scott. Now I knew what was wrong. I had gone crazy. My mind had snapped. For a while there I'd thought *I* was Shell Scott.

But slowly reason filtered into my throbbing head again. I'd had all the mad episodes I cared for this morning, and here was a guy I could get my hands on. He was looking squarely at me now, and if ever a man suddenly appeared scared green, this one did. Except for the short white hair and the fact that he was about my size, he didn't resemble me much, and right now he looked sick. I got up and leaned on the desk and shoved my face at him.

"That's interesting," I said pleasantly. "I, too, am Shell Scott."

He let out a grunt and started to get up fast, but I reached out and grabbed a bunch of shirt and tie and throat in my right fist and I yanked him halfway across the desk.

"O. K., you smart sonofabitch," I said, "Let's have a lot of words. Fast, mister, before I break some bones for you."

He squawked and sputtered and tried to jerk away, so I latched onto him with the other hand and started to haul him over the desk where I could get at him good. I only started to though, because I heard somebody behind me. I twisted my head around just in time to see the pretty boy from Pete's, the guy who'd left the Ladies Room by the window. Just time to see him, and the leather-wrapped sap in his hand, swinging down at me. Then another bomb, a larger one this time, went off in my head and I could feel myself falling, for miles and miles, through deepening blackness.

I came to in front of my desk, and I stayed there for a couple of minutes, got up, made it to the desk chair and sat down in it. If I had thought my head hurt before, it was nothing to the way it felt now. It took me about ten seconds to go from angry to mad to furious to raging, then I grabbed the phone and got Hazel.

"Where'd those two guys go?"

"What guys?"

"You see anybody leave my office?"

"No, Shell. What's the matter?"

"Plenty." I glanced at my watch. Nine-twenty. Just twenty minutes since I'd first opened the office door this morning and answered the ringing phone. I couldn't have been sprawled on the floor more than a minute or two, but even so my two pals would be far away by now. Well, Harrison was going to have a long wait because I was taking no cases but my own for a while. What with people shooting at me, impersonating me, and batting me on the head, this was a mess I had to find out about fast.

"Hazel," I said, "get me the Hollywood Roosevelt."

While I waited I calmed down a little and, though the throbbing in my head made it difficult, my thoughts got a little clearer. It seemed a big white-haired ape was passing himself off as me, but I didn't have the faintest idea why. He must have been down below on Broadway somewhere, waited till he saw me leave, then come up. What I couldn't figure was how the hell he'd known I'd be leaving my office. He certainly couldn't have intended hanging around all day just in case I left, and he couldn't have known I'd be at Pete's . . .

I stopped as a thought hit me. "Hazel," I said. "Forget that call." I hung up, thinking. Whitey couldn't have known I'd show up with a hangover, but he might have known I'd be out of here soon after I arrived. All it takes to get a private detective out of his office is — a phone call. An urgent appointment to meet somebody somewhere, say. Maybe somebody like Frank Harrison. Could be I was reaching for that one, but I didn't think so. I'd had only the one call this morning, an urgent call that would get me out of the office — and from the very guy who'd pulled the same deal last Monday. And all I'd done Monday was waste an hour. The more I thought about it the more positive I became.

Harrison might still be waiting in the Cinegrill — and he might not. If Harrison were in whatever this caper was with Whitey and Pretty Boy, they'd almost surely phone him soon to let him know I hadn't followed the script; perhaps were even phoning him right now. He'd know, too, that unless I was pretty stupid, I'd sooner or later figure out his part in this.

Excitement started building in me as I grabbed my gun and holster and strapped them on; I was getting an inkling of what might have been wrong with that black-haired lovely. Maybe I'd lost Whitey and Pretty Boy, but with luck I could still get my hands on Harrison. Around his throat, say. I charged out of the office. My head hurt all the way but I made it to the lot where I park my convertible Cadillac, leaped in and roared out onto Broadway. From L. A. to downtown Hollywood I broke hell out of the speed limit, and at the hotel I found a parking spot at the side entrance, hurried through the big lobby and into the Cinegrill.

I remembered Harrison was a very tall diplomat-type with hair graying at the temples and bushy eyebrows over dark eyes. Nobody even remotely like him was in the bar. I asked the bartender, "You know a Frank Harrison?"

"Yes, sir."

"He been in here?"

"Yes, sir. He left just a few minutes ago."

"Left the hotel?"

"No, he went into the lobby."

"Thanks." I hustled back into the lobby and up to the desk. A tall, thin clerk in his middle thirties, wearing rimless glasses looked at me when I stopped.

"I've got an appointment with Mr. Frank Harrison," I said. "What room is he in?"

"Seven-fourteen, sir." The clerk looked a little bewildered. "But Mr. Harrison just left."

"Where'd he go? How long ago?"

The clerk shook his head. "He was checking out. I got his card, and when I turned around I saw him going out the door. Just now. It hasn't been a minute. I don't —"

I turned around and ran for the door swearing under my breath. The bastard would have been at the desk when I came in through the side entrance and headed for the Cinegrill. He must have seen me, and that had been all; he'd powdered. He was well powdered, too, because there wasn't a trace of him when I got out onto Hollywood Boulevard.

Inside the hotel again I checked some more with the bartender and desk clerk, plus two bellboys and a dining-room waitress. After a lot of questions I knew Harrison had often been seen in the bar and dining room with two other men. One was stocky, with curly black hair, white skin, cleft chin, quite handsome — Pretty Boy; the other was bigger and huskier and almost always wore a hat. A bellhop said he looked a bit like me. I told him it *was* me, and left him looking bewildered. Two bellboys and the bartender also told me that Harrison was seen every day, almost *all* of every day, with a blonde woman a few years under thirty whom they all described as "stacked." The three men and the blonde were often a foursome. From the bartender I learned that Harrison had got a phone call in the Cinegrill about five minutes before I showed up. That would have been from the other two guys on my list, and fit with Harrison's checking out fast — or starting to. I went back to the desk and chatted some more with the thin clerk after showing him the photostat of my license. Pretty Boy — Bob Foster — was in room 624; Whitey — James Flagg — was in 410; Frank Harrison was in 714.

I asked the clerk, "Harrison married to a blonde?"

"I don't believe he is married, sir."

"He's registered alone?" He nodded, and I said, "I understand he's here a lot with a young woman. Right?"

"Yes, sir. That's Miss Willis."

"A blonde?"

"Yes. Quite, ah, curvaceous."

"What room is she in?"

He had to check. He came back with the card in his hand and said, "Isn't this odd? I had never noticed. She's in seven-sixteen."

It wasn't at all odd. I looked behind him to the slots where room keys were kept. There wasn't any key in the slot for 714. Nor was there any key in the 716 slot. I thanked the clerk, took an elevator to the seventh floor and walked to Harrison's room. There were two things I wanted to do. One was look around inside here to see if maybe my ex-client had left something behind which might help me find him; and the other was to talk with the blonde. As it turned out, I killed two birds with one stone.

The door to 714 was locked, and if I had to I was going to bribe a bellboy to let me in. But, first, I knocked.

It took quite a while, and I had almost decided I'd have to bribe the bellhop, but then there was the sound of movement inside, a muffled voice called something I couldn't understand, and I heard the soft thud of feet coming toward the door. A key clicked in the lock and the door swung open. A girl stood there, yawning, her eyes nearly closed, her head drooping as she stared at approximately the top button of my coat.

She was stark naked. Stark. I had seldom seen *anything* so stark. She had obviously just gotten out of bed, and just as obviously had been sound asleep. She still wasn't awake, because blinking at my chest she mumbled, "Oh, for Christ's sake, John."

Then she turned around and walked back into the room. I followed her, as if hypnotized, automatically swinging the door shut behind me. She was about five-six and close to 130 pounds, and she was shaped like what I sometimes muse about after the third highball. Everybody who had described the blonde, and she was a blonde, had been correct: she was not only "stacked" but "ah, curvaceous." There was no mistaking it, either; the one time a man can be positive that a woman's shape is her own is when she is wearing nothing but her shape, and this gal was really in *dandy* shape. She walked away from me toward a bedroom next to this room, like a gal moving in her sleep.

She walked to the bed and flopped

onto it, pulling a sheet up over her, and I followed her clear to the bed, still coming out of shock, my mind not yet working quite like a well-oiled machine. I managed to figure out that my Frank Harrison was actually named John something. Then she yawned, blinked up at me and said, "Well, for Christ's sake, John, stop staring."

And then she stopped suddenly with her mouth stretching wider and wider and her eyes growing enormous as she stared at me. Then she screamed. Man, she screamed like a gal who had just crawled into bed with seventeen tarantulas. I was certainly affecting people in peculiar fashion this morning. She threw off the sheet, leaped to the floor and lit out for an open door in the far wall, leading into the bathroom, and by now that didn't surprise me a bit.

She didn't make it, though. She was only a yard from me at the start, and I took one step toward her, grabbed her wrist and hung on. She stopped screaming and slashed long red fingernails at my face, but I grabbed her hand and shoved her back onto the bed, then said, "Relax, sister. Stop clawing at me and keep your yap closed and I'll let go of you."

She was tense, jerking her arms and trying to get free, but suddenly she relaxed. Her face didn't relax, though; she still glared at me, a mixture of hate, anger, and maybe fright, staining her face. She didn't have makeup on, but her face had a hard, tough-kid attractiveness.

I let go of her and she grabbed the sheet, pulled it up in front of her body. "Get the hell out of here," she said nastily. There was a phone on a bedside stand and her eyes fell on it. She grabbed it, pulled it off the hook. "I'm calling the cops."

I pulled a chair over beside the bed and sat down. Finally she let go of the phone and glared some more at me.

"I didn't think you'd call any cops, sweetheart," I said. "Maybe I will, but you won't. Quite a shock seeing me here, isn't it? I was supposed to meet Frank — I mean, John — in the Cinegrill, not up here. You're in trouble, baby."

"I don't know what you're talking about."

"Not much. You know who I am —"

"You're crazy."

"Shut up, Miss Willis. I got a call from your boy friend at nine sharp this morning. I was supposed to rush out here for an important job; only there isn't any important job. Your John, the guy I know as Frank Harrison, just wanted me out of my office for an hour or so. Right?"

She didn't say anything.

"So another guy could play Shell Scott for a while. Now you tell me why."

Her lips curled and she swore at me.

I said, "Something you don't know. You must have guessed the caper's gone sour, but you probably don't know John has powdered. Left you flat, honey."

She frowned momentarily, then her face smoothed and got blank. It stayed blank for several minutes and there were a lot of questions she could have answered. She was clammed good. Finally I said, "Look, I know enough of it already. There's John, and Bob Foster, and a big white-haired slob named Flagg who probably got his peroxide from you. And don't play innocent because I know you're thick with all of them, especially John. Hell, this is his room. So get smart and —"

The phone rang. She reached for it, then stopped.

I yanked the .38 out from under my coat and said, "Don't get wise; say hello." I took the phone off the hook and held it for her. She said, "Hello," and I put the phone to my ear just in time to hear a man's voice say, "John, baby. I had to blow fast, that bastard was in the hotel. Pack and meet me at Apex." He stopped.

I covered the mouthpiece and told the blonde, "Tell him O.K. Just that, nothing else."

I stuck the phone up in front of her and she said, "The panic's on. Fade out." I got the phone back to my ear just in time to hear the click as he hung up.

The blonde was smiling at me. But she stopped smiling when I stuck my gun back in its holster, then juggled the receiver and said, "Get me the Hollywood Detective Division."

"Hey, wait a minute," the blonde said. "What you calling the cops for?"

"You can't be that stupid. Tehachapi for you, sweetheart. You probably have a lot of friends there. It won't be so bad. Just horrible."

She licked her lips. When the phone was answered I said, "Put Lieutenant Bronson on, will you?"

The gal said, "Wait a minute. Hold off on that call. Let's . . . talk about it."

I grinned. "Now you want to talk. No soap. You can talk to the cops. And don't tell me there isn't enough to hold you on."

"Please. I . . . call him later if you have to." She let go of the sheet and it fell to her waist. I told myself to be strong and look away, but I was weak.

"You got it all wrong," she said softly. "Let's . . . talk." She tried to smile, but it didn't quite come off. I shook my head.

She threw the sheet all the way back on the bed then, stood up, holding her body erect, and stepped close to me. "Please, honey. We can have fun. Don't you like me, honey?"

"What's with that white-haired ape in my office? And what's Apex?"

"I don't know. I told you before. Honest. Honey, look at me."

That was a pretty silly thing to say, because I sure wasn't looking at the wallpaper. Just then Lieutenant Bronson came on and I said, "Shell Scott here, Bron. Hollywood Roosevelt, room seven-fourteen."

The blonde stepped closer, almost touching me, then picked up my free right hand and passed it around her waist. "Hang up," she said. "You won't be sorry." Her voice dropped lower, became a husky murmur as she pressed my fingers into the warm flesh. "Forget it honey. I can be awfully nice."

Bronson was asking me what was up. I said, "Just a second, Bron," then to the girl, "Sounds like a great kick. Just tell me the story, spill your guts —"

She threw my hand away from her, face getting almost ugly, and then she took a wild swing at me. I blocked the blow with my right hand, put my hand flat on her chest and shoved her back against the bed. She sprawled on it, saying some very nasty things.

I said into the phone, "I've got a brassy blonde here for you."

"What's the score?"

"Frankly, I'm not sure. But I'll sign a complaint. Using foul language, maybe."

"That her? I can hear her."

"Or maybe attempted rape." I grinned at the blonde as she yanked the sheet over her and used some more foul language. I said to Bronson, "Actually, it looks like some kind of confidence game — with me a sucker. I don't know the gal, but you guys might make her. Probably she's got a record." I saw the girl's face change as she winced. "Yeah," I added, "she's got a record. Probably as long as her face is right now."

"I'll send a man up."

"Make it fast, will you? I've got to get out of here, and this beautiful blonde hasn't a stitch of clothes on."

"Huh? She — I'll be right there."

It didn't take him long. By ten-forty-five Bronson, who had arrived grinning — and the three husky sergeants who came with him — had taken the blonde away and I was back in the hotel's lobby. I had given Bronson a rundown on the morning's events, and he'd said they'd keep after the blonde. Neither of us expected any chatter from her, though. After that soft, "I can be awfully nice," she hadn't said anything except swear words and: "I want a lawyer, I know my rights, I want a lawyer." She'd get a lawyer. Tomorrow, maybe.

I went into the Cinegrill and had a bourbon and water while I tried to figure my next move. Bron and I had checked the phone book and city directory for an "Apex" and found almost fifty of them, from Apex Diaper Service to an Apex Junk Yard, which was no help at all, though the cops would check. That lead was undoubtedly no good now that the blonde had warned Harrison. I was getting more and more anxious to find out what the score was, because this was sure shaping up like some kind of con, and I wasn't a bit happy about it.

The confidence man is, in many ways, the elite of the criminal world. Usually intelligent, personable, and more persuasive than Svengali, con-men would be the nicest guys in the world except for one thing: they have no conscience at all. I've run up against con-men before, and they're tricky and treacherous. One of my first clients was an Englishman who had been taken on the rag, a stock swindle, for $140,000. He'd tried to find the man, with no luck, then came to me; I didn't have any luck, either. But when he'd finally given up hope of ever seeing his money again, he'd said to me, of the grifter who had taken him, "I shall always remember him as an extrahdn'rly chahming chap. He was a pleasant bahstahd." Then he'd paused, thought a bit, and added, "But, by God, he *was* a bahstahd!"

The Englishman was right. Confidence men are psychologists with diplomas from sad people: the suckers, the marks, that the con-boys have taken; and there's not a con-man worthy of the name who wouldn't take a starving widow's last penny or a bishop's last C-note, with never a twinge of remorse. They are the pleasant bastards, the con-men, and they thrive because they can make other men believe that opportunity is not only knocking but chopping the door down — and because of men's desire for a fast, even if dishonest, buck, or else the normal greed that's in most of us. They are the spellbinders, and ordinarily don't resort to violence, or go around shooting holes in people.

And it looked as if three of them, or at least two, were up against me. The other one, Pretty Boy Foster, was a bit violent, I remembered, and swung a mean sap. My head still throbbed. All three men, now that the blonde had told Harrison there was big trouble, would probably be making themselves scarce.

But there was still the girl. The gorgeous little gal with black hair and light blue eyes and the chrome-plated pistol. I thought back over what she'd said to me. There'd been a lot of gibberish about $24,000 and my being a crook and . . . something else. Something about Folsom's Market. It was worth a check. I looked the place up in the phone book, found it listed on Van Ness Avenue, finished my drink and headed for Folsom's Market.

It was on Van Ness near Washington. I parked, went inside and looked around. Just an ordinary small store; the usual groceries and a glass-faced meat counter extending the length of the left wall. The place was doing a good business. I walked to the single counter where a young red-haired girl about twenty was ringing up a customer's sales on the cash register, and when she'd finished I told her I wanted to speak with the manager. She smiled, then leaned forward to a small mike and said, "Mr. Gordon. Mr. Gordon, please."

In a few seconds a short man in a business suit, with a fleshy pink face and a slight potbelly walked up to me. I told him my name and business, showed him my credentials, then said, "Actually, Mr. Gordon, I don't know if you can help me or not. This morning I talked briefly with a young lady who seemed quite angry with me. She thought I was some kind of crook and mentioned this place, Folsom's Market. Perhaps you know her." I described the little doll, and she was easy enough to describe, particularly with the odd gray streak in her dark hair. That gal was burned into my memory and I remembered every lovely thing about her, but when I finished the manager shook his head.

"Don't remember anything like her around here," he said.

"She mentioned something about her father, and twenty-four thousand dollars. I don't —"

I stopped, because Mr. Gordon suddenly started chuckling. The cashier said, "Oh, it must be that poor old man."

The manager laughed. "This'll kill you," he said. "Some old foreigner about sixty years old came in here this morning, right at eight when we opened up. Said he just wanted to look his store over. *His* store, get that, Mr. Scott. Claimed he'd bought the place, and — this'll kill you — for twenty-four thousand dollars. Oh, boy, a hundred grand wouldn't half buy this spot."

He was laughing about every third word. It had been very funny, he thought. Only it wasn't a bit funny to me, and I felt sick already. The way this deal was starting to figure, I didn't blame the little cutey for taking a few shots at me.

I said slowly, "Exactly what happened? What else did this . . . this foreigner do?"

The manager's potbelly shook a little. "Ah, he gawked around for a while, then I talked to the guy. I guess it must of taken me half an hour to convince him Mr. Borrage owns this place — you know Borrage, maybe, owns a dozen independent places like this, real rich fellow — anyway this stupid old guy swore he'd bought the place. For the money and his little grocery store. You imagine that? Finally I gave him Borrage's address and told him to beat it. Hell, I called Borrage, naturally. He got a chuckle out of it, too, when I told him."

Anger was beginning to flicker in me. "Who was this stupid old man?" I asked him.

He shrugged. "Hell, I don't know. I just told him finally to beat it. I couldn't have him hanging around here."

"No," I said. "Of course not. He was a foreigner, huh?" You mean he wasn't an Indian?"

Mr. Gordon blinked at me, said, "Hey?" then described the man as well as he could. He told me he'd never seen the guy before, and walked away.

The cashier said softly, "It wasn't like that at all, Mr. Scott. And he left his name with me."

"Swell, honey. Can you give it to me?"

Her face was sober, unsmiling as she nodded. "I just hate that Mr.

Gordon," she said. "The way it was, this little man came in early and just stood around, looking pleased and happy, kind of smiling all the time. I noticed he was watching me for a while, when I checked out the customers, then he came over to me and smiled. 'You're a fast worker,' he said to me. 'Very good worker, I'm watching you.' Then he told me I was going to be working for him, that he'd bought this place and was going to move in tomorrow." She frowned. "I didn't know any better. For all I knew, he might have bought the store. I wish he had." She glanced toward the back of the store where Mr. Gordon had gone. "He was a sweet little man."

"What finally happened?"

"Well, he kept standing around, then Mr. Gordon came up here and I asked him if the store had been sold. He went over and talked to the old man a while, started laughing, and talked some more. The old man got all excited and waved his arms around and started shouting. Finally Mr. Gordon got a little sharp — he's like that — and pointed to the door. In a minute the little guy came over to me and wrote his name and address down. He said there was some kind of mistake, but it would be straightened out. Then he left." She paused. "He looked like he was going to cry."

"I see. You got that name handy?"

"Uh-huh." She opened the cash register and took a slip of paper out of it. "He wanted us to be able to get in touch with him; he acted sort of dazed."

"He would have," I said. She handed me the note. On it, in a shaky, laboriously scrawled script, was written an address and: *Emil Elmlund, Elmlund's Neighborhood Grocery. Phone WI 2-1258.*

"Use your phone?" I asked.

"Sure."

I dialed WI 2-1258. The phone rang several times, then a girl's voice answered, "Hello."

"Hello. Who is this, please?"

"This is Janet Elmlund."

That was what Pretty-Boy had called the girl in Pete's; Janet, and Jan. I said, "Is Mrs. McCurdy there?"

"McCurdy? I — you must have the wrong number."

I told her I wanted WI 2-1259, apologized, and hung up. I didn't want her to know I was coming out there. This time she might have a rifle. Then I thanked the cashier, went out to the Cad and headed for Elmlund's Neighborhood Grocery.

It was a small store on a tree-lined street, the kind of "Neighborhood Grocery" you used to see a lot of in the days before Supermarkets sprang up on every other corner. A sign on the door said, "Closed Today." A path had been worn in the grass alongside the store's right wall, leading to a small house in the rear. I walked along the path and paused momentarily before the house. It was white, neat, with green trim around the windows, a porch along its front. A man sat on the porch in a wooden chair, leaning forward, elbows on his knees, hands clasped. He was looking right at me as I walked toward him, but he didn't give any sign that he'd noticed me, and his face didn't change expression.

I walked up onto the porch. "Mr. Elmlund?"

He slowly raised his head and looked at me. He was a small man, with a lined brown face and very light blue eyes. Wisps of gray hair still clung to his head. He looked at me and blinked, then said, "Yes."

He looked away from me then, out into the yard again. It was as if I weren't there at all. And, actually, my presence probably didn't mean a thing to him. It was obvious that he had been taken in a confidence game, taken for $24,000 and maybe a dream. I couldn't know all of it yet, but I knew enough about how he must feel now, still shocked, dazed, probably not yet thinking at all.

I squatted beside him and said, "Mr. Elmlund, my name is Shell Scott."

For a minute nothing happened, then his eyebrows twitched, pulled down. Frowning, he looked at me. "What?" he said.

I heard the click of high heels, the front door was pushed open and a girl stood there, holding a tray before her with two sandwiches on it. It was the same little lovely, black hair pulled back now and tied with a blue ribbon. She still wore the blue clam-diggers and the man's shirt.

I stood up fast. "Hold everything," I said to her. "Get this through your head — there's a guy in town about my size, with hair the same color as mine, and he's pretending to be me. He's taken my name, and he's used my office. But I never heard of you, or Mr. Elmlund, or Folsom's Market until this morning. Now don't throw any sandwiches at me and for God's sake don't start shooting."

She had been staring at me openmouthed ever since she opened the door and spotted me. Finally her mouth came shut with a click and her hands dropped. The tray fell clattering to the porch and the sandwiches rolled almost to my feet. She stared at me for another half minute without speaking, comprehension growing on her face, then she said, "Oh, no. Oh, my God. Oh, no."

"Oh, yes," I said. "Now suppose we all sit down and get to the bottom of this mess."

She said, "Really? Please . . . you wouldn't —"

"I wouldn't." I showed her several different kinds of identification from my wallet, license, picture, even a fingerprint, and when I finished she was convinced. She blinked those startlingly blue eyes at me and said, "How awful. I'm so sorry. Can you ever forgive me?"

"Yes. Yes, indeed. Right now, I forgive you."

"You don't. You can't." For the first time since I'd seen her, she wasn't looking furious or shocked, and for the moment at least she seemed even to have forgotten about the money they'd lost. I had, I suppose, spoken with almost frantic eagerness, and now she lowered her head slightly and blinked dark lashes once, and her red lips curved ever so slightly in a soft smile. At that moment I could have forgiven her if she'd been cutting my throat with a hack saw. She said again, "You can't."

"Oh, yes I can. Forget it. Could have happened to anybody."

She laughed softly, then her face sobered as she apparently remembered why I was here. I remembered, too, and started asking questions. Ten minutes later we were all sitting on the porch eating picnic sandwiches and drinking beer, and I had most of the story. Mr. Elmlund — a widower, and Janet's father — had run the store here for more than ten years, paid for it, saved $24,000. He was looking for a larger place and had been talking about this to a customer one day, a well-dressed man, smooth-talking, very tall, graying at the temples. The guy's name was William Klein, but he was also apparently my own Frank Harrison. It seemed Harrison was a real-estate broker and had casually mentioned that he'd let Mr. Elmlund know if he ran across anything that looked good.

Mr. Elmlund sipped his beer and kept talking. Elmlund said to me, "He seemed like a very nice man, friendly. Then when he come in and told me about this place it sounded good. He said this woman was selling the store because her husband had died not long ago. She was selling the store and everything and going back East, wasn't really much interested in making a lot of money out of it. She was rich, had a million dollars or more. She just wanted to get away fast, he said, and would sell for sixty thousand cash. Well, I told him that was too much, but he asked me to look at it — that was Folsom's Market — maybe we could work a deal, he said. So the next Sunday we went there; I didn't think it would hurt none to look."

"Sunday? Was the store open?"

"No, it was closed, but he had a key. That seemed right because he was — he said he was agent for it. Well, it was just like I'd always wanted, a nice store. Nice market there, and plenty room, good location . . ." He let the words trail off.

The rest of it was more of the same. The old con play; give the mark a glimpse of something he wants bad, then make him think he can have it for little or nothing, tighten the screws. A good con-man can tie up a mark so tight that normal reasoning powers go out the window. And getting a key which would open the store wouldn't have been any more trouble than getting the one which opened my office.

Last Sunday, a week after they'd looked over the store, Harrison had come to Elmlund all excited, saying the widow was anxious to sell and was going to advertise the store for sale in the local papers. If Elmlund wanted the place at a bargain price he'd have to act fast. Thursday — today, now — the ads would appear and the news would be all over town; right then only the widow, Harrison, and Elmlund himself knew about it. So went Harrison's story. After some more talk Harrison had asked how much cash Elmlund could scrape together. When Harrison learned $24,000 was tops, why naturally that was just enough cash — plus the deed to Elmlund's old store — to maybe swing a fast deal. All con-men are actors, expert at making their lines up as they go along, and Harrison must have made up the bit about throwing the deed in merely to make Elmlund think he was paying a more legitimate price; no well-played mark would think of wondering why a widow getting rid of one store so she could blow would take another as part payment.

Janet broke in, looking at me. "That was when Dad thought about having the transaction investigated. He talked to me about it and decided to see you, have you look into it. You see, he thought the sale was still secret, and you could check on it before the ads came out in the papers. And . . . he just couldn't believe it. He intended originally to invest only about ten thousand above what we'd get out of our store, but, well, it seemed like such a wonderful chance for him, for us. We were both a little suspicious, though."

"Uh-huh." I could see why Elmlund might want the deal checked, and I could even understand why he'd decided to see me instead of somebody else. The last six months I'd been mixed up in a couple cases that got splashed all over the newspapers, and my name was familiar to most of Los Angeles. But another bit puzzled me.

I said, "Janet, this morning in Pete's —" she made a face — "who was the man who charged in and yelled at you? Just as you were . . . leaving."

"Man? I didn't see any man. I . . . lost my head." She smiled slightly. "I guess you know. And after . . . afterwards, I got scared and ran, just wanted to get away. I thought maybe I'd killed somebody."

"I thought maybe you had, myself."

She said, "I was almost crazy. Dad had just told me what had happened, and I was furious. And you'd told Dad everything was fine, that the transaction was on the level — I mean *he* had, that other Shell Scott . . . you know."

"Yeah. What about that?" I turned to Mr. Elmlund. "When did you see this egg in my office?" I already knew, but I wanted to be sure.

"At nine-thirty on Monday morning, this last Monday. I went in right at nine-thirty, there in the Hamilton Building, and talked to him. He said he'd investigate it for me. Then yesterday morning he came out to the store here and said it was all right. It cost me fifty dollars."

"Sure. That made the con more realistic. You'd have thought it was funny if you weren't soaked a little for the job."

He shrugged and said, "Then, right after I talked yesterday to the detective — that one — he drove me and Janet from here to the real-estate office, the Angelus Realty. Said he was going by there. Well, I stopped at the bank — those ads were supposed to come out in the papers today, you know — and got the money. Then at that office I gave them the money and signed all the papers and things and . . . that was all. I wasn't supposed to go to the store till tomorrow, but I couldn't wait."

Janet told me where the "real-estate office" was, on Twelfth Street, but I knew that info was no help now. She said that this morning, before she'd come charging in at me, she'd first gone to the Angelus Realtors — probably planning to shoot holes in Harrison, though she didn't say so. But the place had been locked and she'd then come to the Hamilton Building. She remembered the sign "Angelus Realtors" had still been painted on the door, but I knew, sign or no sign, that office would be empty.

I looked at Janet. "This guy I was talking about, the one in Pete's Bar this A.M., was about five-ten, stocky, I suppose you'd say he was damned good-looking. Black hair, even features."

"That sounds like Bob Foster. Cleft chin and brown eyes?"

"That's him. Did you meet him before or after this deal came up?"

"Bob? Why, you can't think he —"

"I can and do. I'm just wondering which way it was; did he set up the con, or did he come in afterwards."

"Why, I met Bob a month before the realtor showed up. Bob and I went out several times."

"Then dear Bob told him to come around, I imagine. I suppose Bob knew your father was thinking about a new store."

"Yes, but . . ."

"And after you and your father talked about hiring me to make sure the deal was square, did Bob happen to learn about it?"

"Why . . . he was here when we discussed it. He —" she stopped, eyes widening. "I'd forgotten it until now, but *Bob* suggested that dad engage an investigator. When we told him we couldn't believe it, that there just had to be something wrong or dishonest about the sale for the price to be so low, *he* suggested we hire a detective to investigate the man and all the rest of it." She paused again. "He even suggested your name, asked us if we'd heard of you or met you. We hadn't met you, but of course we'd read about you in the papers, and told

Bob so. He said he knew you, that you were capable and thoroughly honest — and he . . . made the appointment with you for nine-thirty Monday."

"Good old Bob," I said. "That made it perfect. That would get rid of the last of your doubts. Janet, Bob Foster is probably no more his right name than Harrison is a real-estate dealer. The guy I know as Harrison, you know as Klein; his girl friend calls him John, and his real name is probably Willie Zilch. And I'm not getting these answers by voodoo. Harrison, Foster, and the guy who said he was Shell Scott all stay at the same hotel. They're a team, with so many fake names they sound like a community."

"But Bob — I thought he was interested in me. He was always nice."

"Yeah, pleasant. So you saw him a few times, and then he learned your dad was ripe for a swindle. He tipped Harrison, the inside-man, and they set up the play. The detective angle just tied it tighter. It was easy enough. A phone call to me to get me out of the office, another guy bleaches his hair, walks in and waits for your dad to show, then kills a couple days and reports all's well."

It was quiet for a minute, then I said, "The thing I don't get is how he happened to show up at Pete's right after you did?"

Mr. Elmlund answered that one. "He and Jan were going on a picnic today. When I told her about — about losing my money she ran to the car and drove away. Right after, Bob come in and asked for Janet. I told him what happened. Said she mentioned going to see that Klein and you. Now I think of it, he got a funny look and run off to his car."

"I hate to say it, Janet," I said, "but Bob was probably less interested in the picnic — under the circumstances — than in finding out if everything was still under control."

I thought a minute. The white-haired egg had probably been planted outside waiting for me to leave; when I did, he went up to the office. Bob must have showed up and checked with Hazel, reached Pete's just as Janet started spraying bullets around, chased her but couldn't find her or else knew he'd better tip Whitey fast. So he'd charged to the office just in time to sap me. Something jarred my thoughts there. It bothered me but I couldn't figure out what it was.

I said, "Have you been to the police yet?"

Janet said, "No. We've been so . . . upset. We haven't done anything since I got back home."

"I'll take care of it, then." I got up. "That's about it, I guess. I'll try running the men down, but it's not likely they'll be easily found. I'll do what I can."

Janet had been sitting quietly, looking at me. Now she got up, took my hand, and pulled me after her into the front room of the house. Inside, she put a hand on my arm and said softly, "You know how sorry I am about this morning. I was a little crazy for a while there. But I want to thank you for coming out, saying you'll help."

"I'll be helping myself, too, Janet."

"I get sick when I think I might actually have shot you." She looked at the raw spot on my chin. "Did I . . . shoot you there?"

I grinned at her. "It might have been a piece of glass. I landed in some."

"Just a minute." She went away and came back with a bit of gauze and a piece of tape. She pressed it gently against the "wound," as she called it, her fingers cool and soft against my cheek. Her touch sent a tingle over my skin, a slight shiver between my shoulder blades. Then she stretched up and gently pressed her lips against my cheek.

"That better?"

It's funny; some women can leap into your lap, practically strangle you, mash their mouth all over you, kiss you with their lips and tongues and bodies, and leave you cold — I'm talking about *you*, of course. But just the gentle touch of this gal's lips on my cheek turned my spine to spaghetti. That was the fastest fever I ever got; a thermometer in my mouth would have popped open and spouted mercury every which way.

I said, "Get your .22. I'm about to shoot myself full of holes."

She laughed softly, her arms going around my neck, then she started to pull herself up but my head was already on its way down, and when her lips met mine it was a new kind of shock. The blonde back there in the hotel room had been fairly enjoyable, but Janet had more sex and fire and hunger in just her lips than the blonde had in her entire stark body. When Jan's hands slid from my neck and she stepped back I automatically moved toward her, but she put a hand on my chest, smiling, glanced toward the porch, then took my arm and led me outside again.

When my breathing was reasonably normal I said, "Mr. Elmlund, I'm leaving now but if I get any news at all, I'll hurry back — I mean, ha, come back."

Janet chuckled. "Hurry's all right," she said.

Mr. Elmlund said, "Mr. Scott, if you can get our money again I'll pay you anything — half of it —"

"Forget that part. I don't want any money. If I should miraculously get it back, it's all yours."

He looked puzzled. "Why? Why should you help me?"

I said, "Actually, Mr. Elmlund, this is just as important to me. I don't like guys using my name to swindle people; I could get a very nasty reputation that way. Not to mention my dislike for being conned myself and getting hit over the head. For all I know there are guys named Shell Scott all over town, conning people, maybe shooting people. The con worked so well for these guys once, they'll probably try the same angles again — or would have if I hadn't walked in . . . on . . ." I stopped. That same idea jarred my thoughts as it had before when I'd been thinking about the guy in my office. It was so simple I should have had it long ago. But now a chill ran down my spine and I leaned toward Mr. Elmlund.

"You weren't supposed to see me — the detective — this morning were you?"

"Why, no. Everything was finished, he already give me his report."

I didn't hear the rest of what he said. I was wondering why the hell Harrison had called me again, why Whitey had needed my office again, if not for Mr. Elmlund.

I swung toward Janet. "Where's your phone? Quick."

She blinked at me, then turned and went into the house. I followed, right on her heels.

"Show me. Hurry."

She pointed out the phone on a table and I grabbed it, dialed the Hamilton Building. There was just a chance — but it was already after noon.

Hazel came on. "This is Shell. Anyone looking for me?"

"Hi, Shell. How's your hangover —"

"This is important, hell with the hangover. Anybody there right after I took off."

Her voice got brisk. "One man, about fifty, named Carl Strossmin. Said he had an appointment for nine-thirty."

"He say what about?"

"No. I took his name and address. Thirty-six, twenty-two Gramercy. Said he'd phone back; he hasn't called."

"Anything else?"

"That's all."

"Thanks." I hung up. I said aloud, "I'll be goddamned. They've got another mark."

Jan said, "What?" but I was running for the door. I leaped into the Cad, gunned the motor and swung around in a U-turn. It was clear enough. Somewhere the boys had landed another sucker, and the "investigation" by Shell Scott had worked so well once that they must have used the gimmick again. They would still be around, but if they made this score they'd almost surely be off for Chicago, or Buenos Aires, or God knew where.

Carl Strossmin — I remembered hearing about him. He'd made a lot of money, most of it in deals barely this side of the law; he'd be the perfect mark because he was always looking for the best of it. Where Elmlund had thought he was merely getting an amazing piece of good fortune, Strossmin might well think he was throwing the blocks to somebody else. I didn't much like what I'd heard about Strossmin, but I liked not at all what I knew of Foster and Whitey and Harrison.

When I spotted the number I wanted on Gramercy I slammed on the brakes, jumped out and ran up to the front door of 3622. I rang the bell and banged on the door until a middle-aged woman looked out at me, frowning.

"Say," she said. "What is the matter with you?"

"Mrs. Strossmin?"

"Yes."

"Your husband here?"

Her eyes narrowed. "No. Why? What do you want him for?"

I groaned. "He isn't closing any business deal, is he?"

Her eyes were slits now. "What are you interested for?" She looked me up and down. "They told us there were other people interested. You —"

"Lady, listen. He isn't buying a store, or an old locomotive or anything, is he?"

She pressed her lips together. "I don't think I'd better say anything till he gets back."

"That's fine," I said. "That's great. Because the nice businessmen are crooks. They're confidence men, thieves, they're wanted by police of seventy counties. Kiss your cabbage goodbye, lady — or else start telling me about it fast."

Her lips weren't pressed together any more. They peeled apart like a couple of liver chunks. "Crooks?" she groaned. "*Crooks?*"

"Crooks, gyps, robbers, murderers. Lady, they're dishonest."

She let out a wavering scream and threw her hands up in the air. "Crooks!" she wailed. "I told him they were crooks. Oh, I told the old fool, you can bet —!" She fainted.

I swore nastily, jerked the screen door open and picked her up, then carried her to a couch. Finally she came out of it and blinked at me. She opened her mouth.

I said, "If you say 'crooks' once again I'll bat you. Now where the hell did your husband go?"

She started babbling, not one word understandable. But finally she got to her feet and started tottering around. "I wrote it down," she said. "I wrote it down. I wrote —"

"What did you write down?"

"Where he was going. The address." She threw up her hands. "Forty-one thousand dollars! Crooks! Forty-one —"

"Listen," I said. "He have that much money on him?"

"No. He had to go to the bank."

"What bank?" By the time she answered I'd already spotted the phone and was dialing. A bank clerk told me that Carl Strossmin had drawn $41,000 out of his account only half an hour ago. He'd been very excited, but he'd made no mention of what he wanted the money for. I hung up. I knew why Carl hadn't mentioned anything about it: it was a secret.

Mrs. Strossmin was still puttering around, pulling out drawers and occasionally throwing her hands up into the air and screeching. Gradually I got her story and, with what I already knew, put the pieces together. Her husband's appointment with "Shell Scott" had been made two days ago by real-estate dealer

"Harrison" himself, here in Strossmin's home. After suggesting that since Strossmin seemed a bit undecided he might feel safer if he engaged a "completely honest" detective, Harrison had dialed a number, chatted a bit, and handed Strossmin the phone. Finally an appointment had been made for nine-thirty this a.m. Strossmin had been talking, of course, to Whitey who most likely was in a phone booth or bar.

Harrison probably wouldn't have suggested me *by name* to Strossmin, expecting the mark to accept his, the realtor's, suggestion, except for one thing, which was itself important to the con: my reputation in L.A. A lot of people here believe I'm crazy, others think I'm stupid, and many, particularly old maids, are sure I'm a fiendish lecher; but there's never been any question about my being honest. This phase of the con was based on making Strossmin — and Elmlund before him — think he was really talking to me when he met Whitey, the Shell Scott of the con, in my office. However when I popped back into the office and messed up that play this morning, the boys had to change their plans fast.

At eleven-thirty, about the time I was driving to Elmlund's, Whitey had come here to Strossmin's home, apologized for not being in his office when Strossmin had arrived this A.M., and said he'd come here to spare Strossmin another trip downtown. After learning what Strossmin wanted investigated, Whitey had pretended surprise and declared solemnly that this was a strange coincidence indeed, because Strossmin was the second man to ask for the identical investigation. Oh, yes, he'd already investigated — for this other eager buyer — and told him that the deal was on the level. No doubt about it, this was the opportunity of the century — and time, sad to say, was terribly short. Apparently, said Whitey, negotiations were going on with dozens of other people — and so on until Strossmin had been in a frenzy of impatience.

Finally Mrs. Strossmin found her slip of paper and thrust it at me. An address was scribbled on it: Apex Realtors, 4870 Normandie Avenue. I grabbed the paper and ran to the Cad.

Apex Realtors was, logically enough, no more than an ordinary house with a sign in the window: Apex Realtors. When I reached it and parked, a small, well-dressed man with a thick mustache was just climbing into a new Buick at the curb. I ran from the Cad to his Buick and stopped him just as he started the engine.

"Mr. Strossmin?"

He was just like his wife. His eyes narrowed. "Yes."

I took a deep breath and blurted it out: "Did you just buy Folsom's Market?"

He grinned. "Beat you, didn't I? You're too late —"

"Shut up. You bought nothing but a headache. How many men inside there?"

He chuckled. "They told me I'd have to hurry. Sorry, my good man, but —"

About ready to flip, I yanked out my gun and pointed it at him. "*How many men in there?*"

I thought for a minute he was going to faint, too, but he managed to gasp, "Three."

I said, "You wait here," then turned and ran up to the house. The door was partly ajar, and I hit it and charged inside, the gun in my right hand. There wasn't anybody in sight, but another door straight ahead of me had a sign, "Office," on it. As I went through the door a car motor growled into life behind the house. I ran for the back, found a door standing wide open and jumped through it just as a sky-blue Oldsmobile sedan parked in the alley took off fast. I barely got a glimpse of it, but I knew who was in it. The three con-men were powdering now that they had all the dough they were after. There was a chance they'd seen me, but it wasn't likely. Probably they'd grabbed the dough and left by the back way as soon as Strossmin stepped through the front door.

I raced out front again and sprinted for the Cad, yelling to Strossmin, "Call the police!" He sat there, probably feeling pleased at the coup he'd just put over. He'd call the cops, next week, maybe. I ripped the Cad into gear and roared to the corner, took a right and stepped on the gas. I had to slow at the next intersection, looked both directions and caught a flash of blue two blocks away on my right, swung in after them and pushed the accelerator to the floorboards. I was gaining on them rapidly, and now I had a few seconds to try figuring out how to stop them. Up close I could see the Olds sedan, and the figures of three men inside it, two in the front seat and one in back. Con-men don't usually carry guns, but these guys operated a little differently from most con-men. In the first place they usually make the mark think he's in on a crooked deal, and in the second they almost always try to cool the mark out, allay his suspicions so he doesn't know, at least for a long time, that he's been taken. The boys ahead of me had broken both those rules, and there was a good chance they'd also broken the rule about guns.

But I was less than half a block behind them now and they apparently hadn't tumbled. They must figure they were in the clear, so I had surprise on my side. Well, I'd surprise them.

We were a long way from downtown here, but still in the residential section. I caught up with their car, pulled out on their left and slightly ahead, then as we reached an intersection I swung to my right, cutting them off just as I heard one of the men in the blue Olds yell loudly.

The driver did the instinctive

thing, jerked his steering wheel to the right and they went clear up over the curb and stalled on a green lawn before a small house. I was out of my Cad and running toward them, the Colt in my fist, before their car stopped moving twenty feet from me. And one of them *did* have a gun.

They sure as hell knew who I was by now, and I heard the gun crack. A slug snapped past me as I dived for the lawn, skidded a yard. Doors swung open on both sides of the blue Olds. Black-haired Pretty Boy jumped from the back and started running away from me, lugging a briefcase.

I got to my knees, and yelled, "Stop! Hold it or you get it, Foster."

He swung around, crouching, and light gleamed on the metal of a gun in his hand. He fired once at me and missed, and I didn't hold back any longer. I snapped the first shot from my .38 but I aimed the next two times, and he sagged slowly to his knees, then fell forward on his face.

Gray-haired Harrison was a few steps from the car, standing frozen, staring at Foster's body, but Whitey was fifty feet beyond him running like mad. I took out after him, but as I went by Harrison I let him have the full weight of my .38 on the back of his skull. I didn't even look back; he'd keep for a while.

I jammed my gun into its holster and sprinted down the sidewalk, Whitey half a block ahead but losing ground. He wasn't in very good shape, apparently, and after a single block he was damn near staggering. He heard my feet splatting on the pavement behind him and for a moment he held his few yards' advantage, then he slowed again. He must have known I had him, because he stopped and whirled around to face me, ready to go down fighting.

He went down, all right, but not fighting. When he stopped I had been less than ten feet from him, traveling like a fiend, and he spun around just in time to connect his face with my right fist. I must have started the blow from six feet away, just as he began turning, and what with my speed from running, and the force of the blow itself, my fist must have been traveling fifty miles an hour.

It was awful what it did to him. I caught only a flashing glimpse of his face as he swung around, lips peeled back and hands coming up, and then my knuckles landed squarely on his mouth and his lips really peeled back and he started going the same direction I was going and almost as fast. I ran several steps past him before I could stop, but when I turned around he was practically behind me and there was a thin streak of blood for two yards on the sidewalk. He was all crumpled up, out cold, and for a minute I thought he was out for good. But I felt for his heartbeat and found it.

So I squatted by him and waited. Before he came out of it, a little crowd gathered: half a dozen kids and some housewives, one young guy about thirty who came running from half a block away. I told him to call the cops and he phoned. Whitey was still out when the guy came back and said a car was on its way.

Finally Whitey stirred, moaned. I looked around and said to the women, "Get the kids out of here. And maybe you better not stick around yourselves."

The women frowned, shifted uneasily, but they shooed the kids away. Whitey shook his head. Finally he was able to sit up. His face wasn't pretty at all. I grabbed his coat and pulled him close to me.

I said, "Shell Scott, huh? I hear you're a tough baby. Get up, friend."

I stood up and watched him while he got his feet under him. It took him a while, and all the time he didn't say a word. I suppose the decent thing would have been to let him get all the way up, but I didn't wait. When he was halfway up I balled my left fist and slammed it under his chin. It straightened him just enough so I could set myself solidly, and get him good with my right fist. It landed where I wanted it to, on his nose, and he left us for a while longer. He fell onto the grass on his back, and perhaps he had looked a bit like me at one time, but he didn't any more.

The guy who had called the cops helped me carry Whitey back to the blue Oldsmobile. We dumped him and Harrison inside and I climbed in back with them — and with the briefcase — while he went out to the curb and waited for a prowl car. I got busy. When I finished, these three boys had very little money in their wallets and none was in the briefcase. It added up to $67,500. There was Elmlund's $24,000, I figured, plus Strossmin's $41,000, plus my $2500. I lit a cigarette and waited for the cops.

It was two p.m. before I got away. Both cops in the patrol car were men I knew well; Borden and Lane. Lane and I especially were good friends. I gave my story and my angles to Lane, and finally he went along with what I wanted.

I finished it with, "This Strossmin is still so wound up by these guys he'll probably figure it out about next week, but when he does, he should be a good witness. No reason why Elmlund can't be left out of it."

Lane shook his head and rubbed a heavy chin where bristles were already sprouting. "Well . . . if this Strossmin doesn't come through in court, we'll need Elmlund."

"You'll get him. Besides, I'll be in court, remember. Enjoying myself."

He nodded. "O.K., Shell."

I handed him the briefcase with $41,000 inside it, told him I'd come to Headquarters later, and took off. I'd given Lane the address where I'd left Strossmin, as well as his home address, but Strossmin hadn't waited. I drove to his house.

I could hear them going at it hammer and tongs. Mrs. Strossmin didn't even stop when I rang the bell, but finally her husband opened the door. He just stood there glowering at me. "Well?" he said.

"I just wanted to let you know, Mr. Strossmin, that the police have caught the men who tricked you."

I was going on, but he said, "Trick me? Nobody tricked me. *You're* trying to trick me."

"Look, mister, I just want you to know your money's safe. The cops have it. My name is Shell Scott —"

"Ha!" he said. "It is, hey? No, it's not, that's not your name, can't fool me. You're a crook, that's what you are."

His wife was in the door.

She screeched in his ear, "What did I say? Old fool, I warned you."

"Mattie," he said. "If you don't sit down and shut up . . ."

I tried some more, but he just wouldn't believe me. A glowing vision could have appeared in the sky crying, "You been tricked, Strossmin!" and the guy wouldn't have believed it. There are marks like him, who beg to be taken.

So finally I said, "Well, you win."

"What?"

"You win. Nothing I can do about it now. Store's yours." I put on a hangdog look. He cackled.

I said, "You can take over the place today, you know. Well, goodbye — and the better man won."

"Today?"

"Yep. Folsom's Market, isn't it?"

"Yes, yes."

"Well, you go right down there. Ask for Mr. Gordon."

"Mr. Gordon?"

"Yep." I shook his hand. He cackled. and Mrs. Strossmin screeched at him, and he told her to shut up and I left. They were still going at it as I drove away to the Elmlunds.

Mr. Elmlund didn't quite know what to do when I dropped the big packet of bills on his table and said the hoods were in the clink. He stared at the money for a long time. When finally he did speak it was just, "I don't know what to say."

Jan came out onto the porch and I told them what happened and I thought they were going to crack up for a while, and then I thought they were going to float off over the trees, but finally Mr. Elmlund said, "I must pay you, Mr. Scott. I must."

I said, "No. Besides, I got paid."

Jan was leaning against the side of the door, smiling at me. She'd changed clothes and was wearing a smooth, clinging print dress now, and the way she looked I really should have had on dark glasses. She looked happy, wonderful, and her light blue eyes were half-lidded, her gaze on my mouth.

"No," she said. "You haven't been paid."

Her tongue traced a smooth, gleaming line over her lower lip, and I remembered her fingers on my cheek, her lips against my skin.

"You haven't been paid, Shell."

I had a hunch she was right.

Get the jewels, Ernie told Del, and keep your hands off the woman. But Del decided that he'd take both.

BY ARNOLD MARMOR

Heirloom

Ernie Speers braked the jalopy to a sudden halt and nodded toward a run-down house partly hidden by magnolia and pecan trees. His fat face was sweating and he sounded out of breath, as if we had been running all the way instead of riding.

"There," he said. "That's where she lives, Del."

I flipped my cigarette through the window and took a good look at the house.

"You've got a gun, haven't you? We made an agreement, didn't we?"

"Yeah."

"Okay, then. I paid your fare from Baton Rouge, and I gave you a hundred bucks on account. All you got to do is get that necklace for me."

I laughed at him. "That's all I have to do, eh, Ernie?"

"You said she'd be alone," I told him. "What if she isn't? What if she's got company?"

He wiped the sweat off his face with the back of his hand. "Forget it," he said. "Nobody ever comes out here." He tapped his forehead with a stubby finger. "Lois Webb is a little touched, Del."

"All right. So she's off, and nobody comes around. But what if she gets any funny notions about hanging onto the necklace?"

"Listen. I'd do this myself, only she knows me. Everybody in this hick town knows me. Why do you think I had to hire you, muscle man?"

I climbed out of the car. "Relax," I told him. "If the stuff's there, I'll get it. One way or another."

He leaned across the seat and shoved his face close to the window. "Remember, Del — you aren't to touch her."

"I'll remember. I'll remember."

"Just get the necklace and come right back. Don't get any ideas, just because she's pretty."

"Sure," I said. I turned then and walked up the path to the house.

Lois Webb was sitting in a chair on the patio. Ernie had said she was pretty, but he hadn't told the half of it. She was young and beautiful and blonde, and her figure was enough to make a man hurt.

She didn't look bugs. Not a bit.

"Hi," I said.

She smiled. "Hello."

"Damn hot, isn't it?"

"Yes." She gave me a long slow look, all the way up and down, as if she liked what she saw.

"I wonder if I could trouble you for a drink of water?" I asked.

She gave me another one of those looks, and then she got to her feet and opened the screen door. "Come in."

I followed her into the kitchen and waited while she filled a glass at the sink. When she turned around, I took the glass out of her hand and put it down on the drainboard, and then I let her see the gun.

She didn't say anything. Her blue eyes widened a little, and she took a quick breath, but that was all.

"Where's the necklace?" I asked.

She fooled me; she didn't try to hedge. She just looked from my face to the gun, and back again, and said, "It's upstairs. In the bedroom."

"Let's get it. All right?"

I followed her up the stairs. They were steep stairs, and her skirt was very short. Those legs were almost too good to be true. By the time we'd reached the top, I was sweating worse than Ernie Speers had been.

She was a smart girl. She didn't stall — even after we got into the bedroom. She went straight to a dresser and dug the necklace out of a drawer and handed it to me.

"It's an heirloom," she said. "My mother's . . ." She had an unusual voice. Very husky. I got the idea she wasn't thinking too much about the pearls. It was wacky, but I got the idea she was thinking about the same thing I was.

I tried the pearls on my teeth, anyhow, just to make sure. They were the McCoy.

I dropped the necklace in my pocket and stood looking at Lois Webb. She took a step toward me, then another. One look at that smile on her face and you knew the score. I didn't have any doubts now about what she was thinking. I reached out for her.

She came to me so fast and hard that for a moment I almost lost my balance. She yanked my head down and mashed her open mouth against mine — and for about twenty seconds the room went around like a pin wheel.

I ran out of breath and started to push her away. But she wouldn't have it. She caught my lower lip between her teeth and bit until I tasted the salty flow of blood.

And all this time, she was moaning

and trembling, and the body beneath was soft and smooth.

Suddenly she moved back from me. She held her arms straight down, the hands balled up into little fists, and her eyes were shut tight. She just stood there, making funny sounds in her throat, and trembling, and then she reached up and ripped her dress all the way to the waist.

There was nothing under the dress. She stood there naked for a second and the next thing I knew, the dress was on the floor and Lois Webb was pulling me to the bed.

Ernie Speers' car was still waiting, and Ernie's fat face was still sweating.

I slid in beside him and patted my pocket. "I got it," I said.

He nodded and reached over to the glove compartment and took out a little leather bag, the kind kids use for marbles.

"Just slip it in here," he said.

I put the pearls in the bag and looked at him. "What's the idea?"

"Safety first," he said. "You remembered? You didn't touch her?"

"So I touched her. So what?" He knew any man would have done everything with a girl like Lois Webb.

His face was suddenly as white as a fish's belly, and his little pig eyes were the sickest eyes I'd ever seen. I thought he was going to vomit.

"What the hell's the difference?"

I don't know where he got it from, but all at once he jammed a gun in my ribs. "Get out of here!"

I looked at the gun. I didn't say anything. I started to get out.

"You crazy bastard!" Ernie said. His voice was high now, almost hysterical. "I told you not to touch her. I told you! I knew you wouldn't do the job if you knew the truth."

I kept looking at the gun. He was leaving me stranded in the middle of nowhere. He had the drop on me.

"I feel sorry for you," Ernie said. "You bastard, you've had it."

"What . . ." I said.

"Why do you think nobody goes near her? Every guy around here knows she's crazy for a man."

I looked at him.

"It's because they're afraid of her," he said. "And all they can do is stay away from her until the Health Officer comes this Saturday."

I lost interest in the gun. I lost interest in everything but what he'd just said. Something cold and hard began to twist around in my stomach, and then he lifted the gun and shouted, "Get the hell out!"

I got out and he slammed the door.

"Health Officer?" I said, half-knowing what his answer would be. "Why . . . the Health Officer?"

Ernie gunned the motor and the car shot ahead. Over his shoulder, and over the roar of the engine, he shouted, "Lois Webb's a *leper*, you damn fool! She's got leprosy!"

And then there was only the cloud of dust behind the disappearing car. That, and the quiet road ringing with the echo of Ernie's words.

MUGGED AND PRINTED

You never know what to expect in a Fredric Brown book. His first book, *The Fabulous Clipjoint*, was laid in Chicago's underworld; the action in his second, *The Dead Ringer*, took place on a traveling carnival. *Murder Can Be Fun* mixed murder with the writers, actors, and producers of a radio show, and the recent *Space On My Hands* was a collection of science-fiction. Brown was born back in 1906 in Cincinnati, and has kicked around since at such jobs as stenographer, insurance salesman, book-keeper, stock clerk, dishwasher, busboy, and — an amazing occupation for a mystery writer — detective. While working as a proofreader in 1940, Brown wondered if he couldn't do better than some of the pulp stories he was reading. He supplied his own answer by selling several hundred and then copping an MWA award for the best mystery.

Frank Kane is a law graduate of St. John's University, class of 1932. Since then, he's had a varied and versatile career: reporter, radio producer, Broadway columnist, public relations expert, and now publisher of his own liquor journals. Before turning to magazine and novel writing, he spent years in radio (which he claims were "ulcer-forming," though he escaped without any) writing *Gangbusters*, *The Shadow*, *Mr. Keen*, *Counter-Spy*, *The Fat Man*, *Nick Carter*, and *Casey, Crime Photographer* to list a few. The Johnny Liddell featured in *Evidence* in this issue has now romped through *Green Light For Death*, *Dead Weight*, *Bare Trap*, *Bullet Proof*, and *Slay Ride*. Frank resides in Manhasset, L. I., where he shares a sprawling home with his wife and three daughters. His background provides a wide selection of material from which he can draw.

Bruno Fischer once wrote in answer to a biography request: "I know how they're supposed to go. A writer's autobiography traditionally consists of the writer and his dog. I can't quite oblige. Not that there isn't a dog in our household, a little black mutt named Maxine, who is seven and unlovely and stupid. But she doesn't sit at my feet as I write. She wouldn't dare." He neglected to mention that his home also contained copies of some of the best mysteries ever penned — and that he'd written them. These include *The Paper Circle*, *The Silent Dust*, *The Restless Hands* — and a vacant spot on the shelf will now be filled with *Say Goodbye To Janie*, which is in this issue. Although Fischer works at home, he sticks to a typical office schedule by keeping the typewriter going from nine to five. He lives in up-state New York along the Hudson.

Craig Rice tells us that a British magazine once wrote her publishers, asking for biographical material on Michael Venning. Since this is one of her well-known pennames, the request was turned over to her. She supplied the magazine with a picture of herself in a deerstalker cap, complete with pipe and false beard. She also gave them a straight picture of Craig Rice, saying that this was Venning's wife, a detective-story writer. To top it all, she sent a picture of her daughter, saying it was Daphne Sanders (another of her pennames), "who has also written a detective novel." Payoff: the British mag ran the complete item, deadpan. *Quiet Day In the County Jail* is a completely different type of story from any of Miss Rice's yarns which feature John J. Malone. But it's a fine, offtrail mood piece with an exciting power-packed punch.

The Fiction House Press Replica Line is available at www.FictionHousePress.com

www.ingramcontent.com/pod-product-compliance
Lightning Source LLC
LaVergne TN
LVHW090958080826
845145LV00003B/1054

* 9 7 8 1 6 4 7 2 0 6 7 0 3 *